The Misadventures of
SALEM HYDE
4

Dinosaur Dilemma

Frank Cammuso

AMULET BOOKS
NEW YORK

PUBLISHER'S NOTE: This is a work of fiction. Names, characters, places, and incidents are either the product of the author's imagination or are used fictitiously, and any resemblance to actual persons, living or dead, business establishments, events, or locales is entirely coincidental.

Hardcover ISBN: 978-1-4197-1534-1
Paperback ISBN: 978-1-4197-1535-8

Text and illustrations copyright © 2015 Frank Cammuso
Book design by Frank Cammuso and Alyssa Nassner

Published in 2015 by Amulet Books, an imprint of ABRAMS.
All rights reserved. No portion of this book may be reproduced, stored in a retrieval system, or transmitted in any form or by any means, mechanical, electronic, photocopying, recording, or otherwise, without written permission from the publisher.

Amulet Books and Amulet Paperbacks
are registered trademarks of Harry N. Abrams, Inc.

Printed and bound in China
10 9 8 7 6 5 4 3 2 1

Amulet Books are available at special discounts when purchased in quantity for premiums and promotions as well as fundraising or educational use. Special editions can also be created to specification. For details, contact specialsales@abramsbooks.com or the address below.

ABRAMS
THE ART OF BOOKS SINCE 1949

115 West 18th Street
New York, NY 10011
www.abramsbooks.com

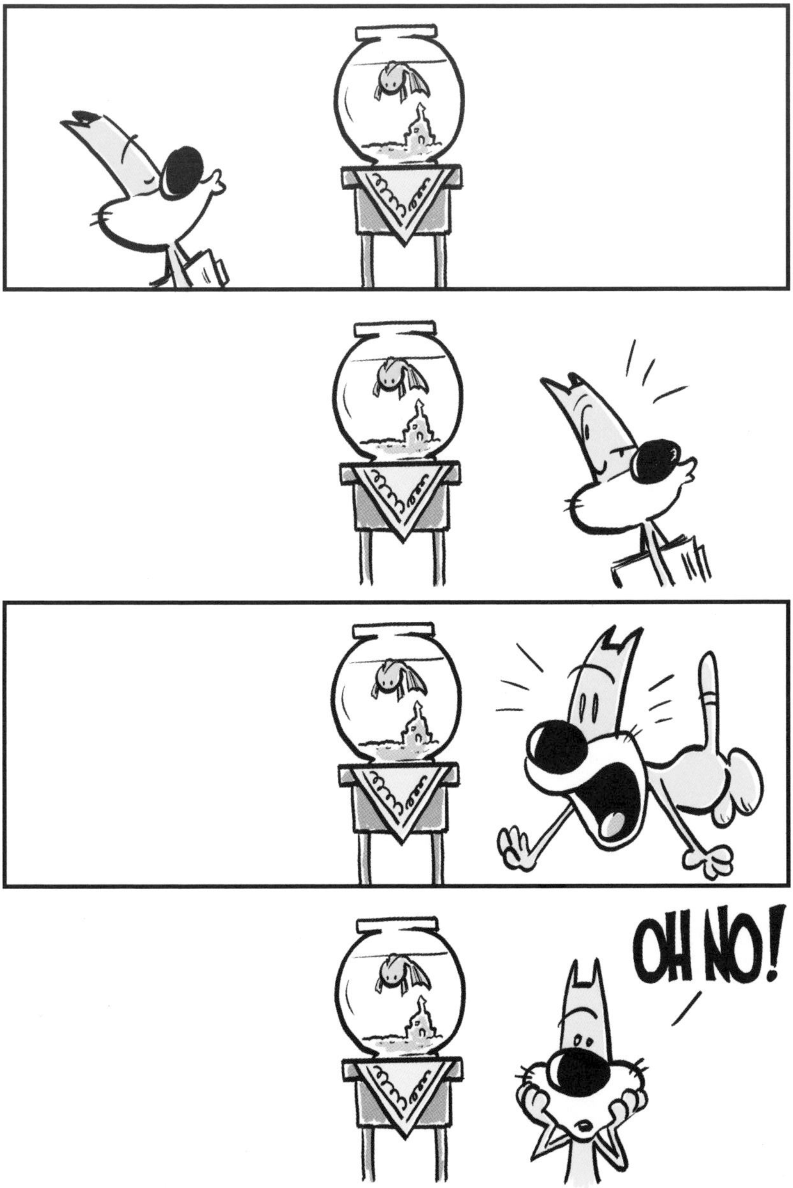
OH NO!

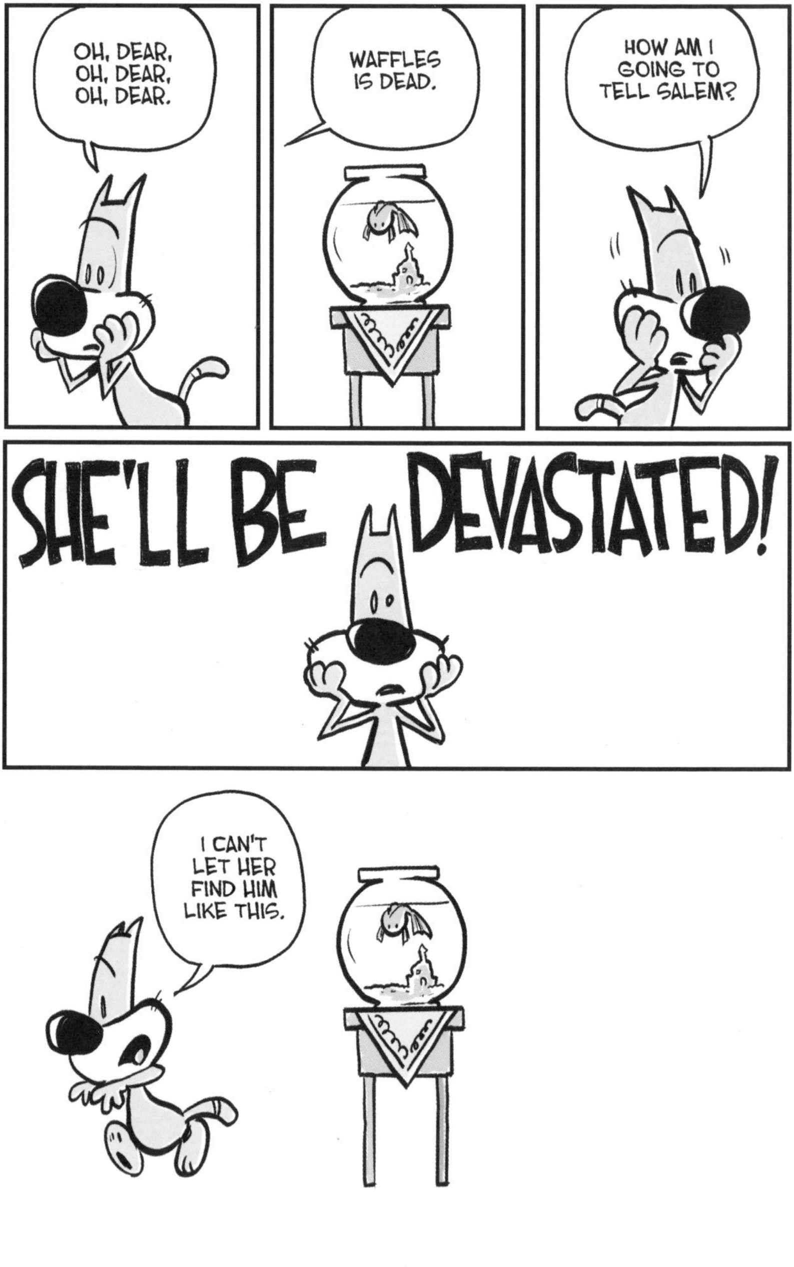
OH, DEAR,
OH, DEAR,
OH, DEAR.
WAFFLES
IS DEAD.
HOW AM I
GOING TO
TELL SALEM?
SHE'LL BE DEVASTATED!
I CAN'T
LET HER
FIND HIM
LIKE THIS.

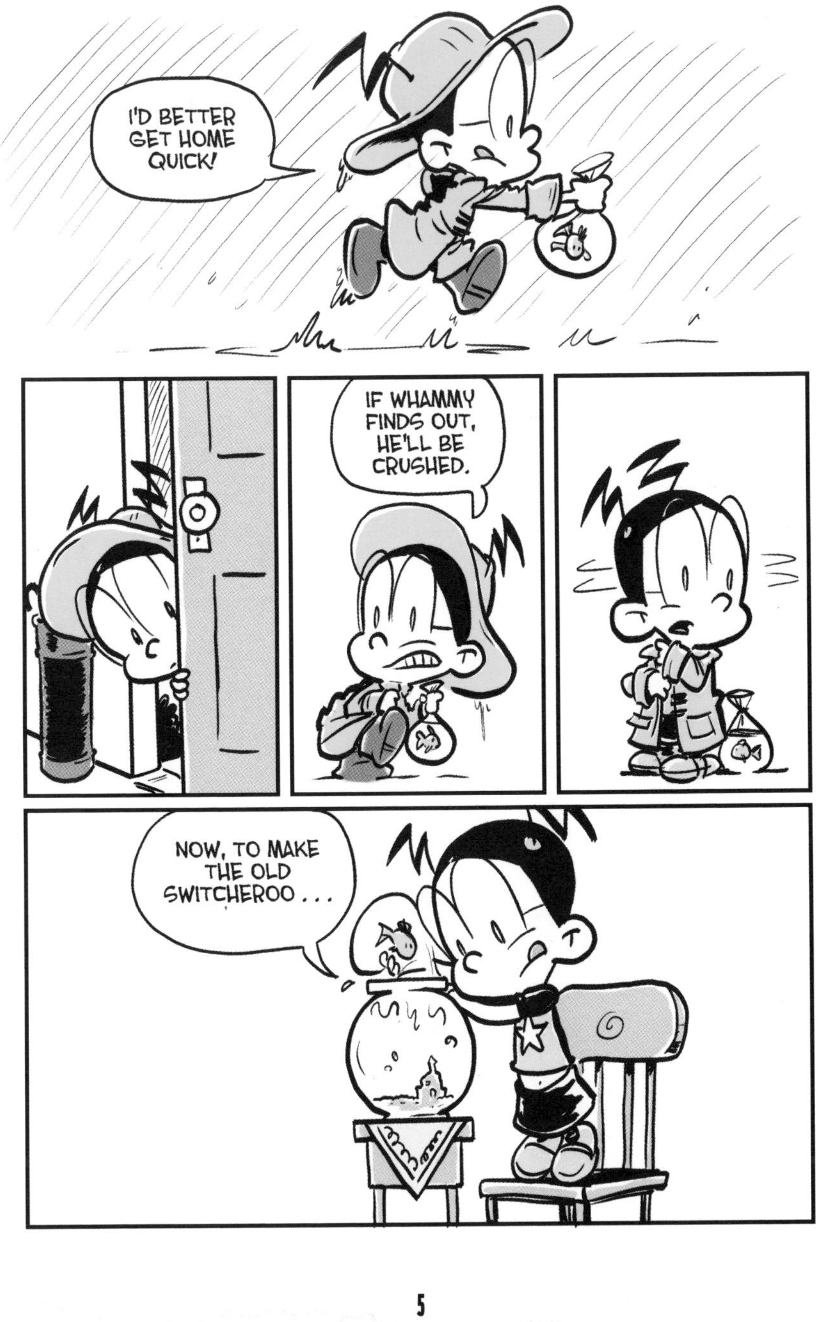
I'D BETTER GET HOME QUICK!
IF WHAMMY FINDS OUT, HE'LL BE CRUSHED.
NOW, TO MAKE THE OLD SWITCHEROO . . .

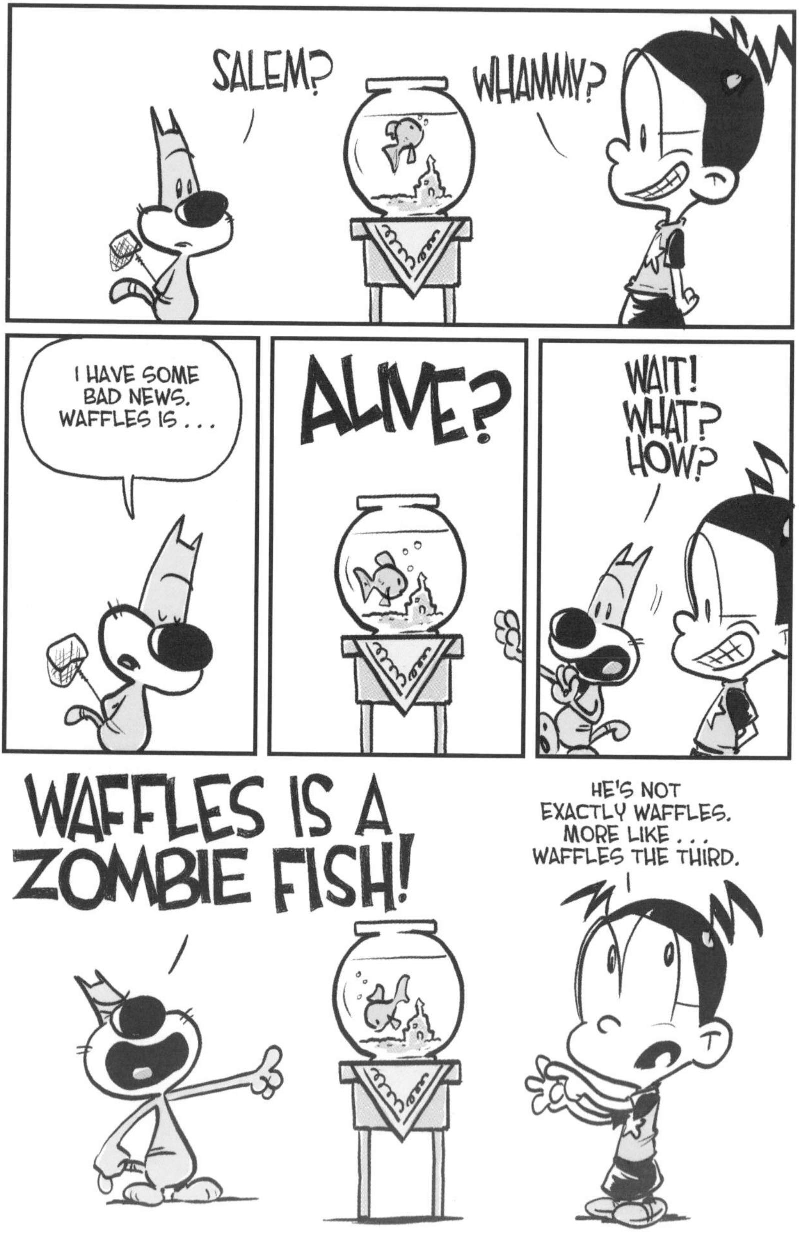
SALEM?
WHAMMY?
I HAVE SOME BAD NEWS. WAFFLES IS . . .
ALIVE?
WAIT! WHAT? HOW?
WAFFLES IS A ZOMBIE FISH!
HE'S NOT EXACTLY WAFFLES. MORE LIKE . . . WAFFLES THE THIRD.

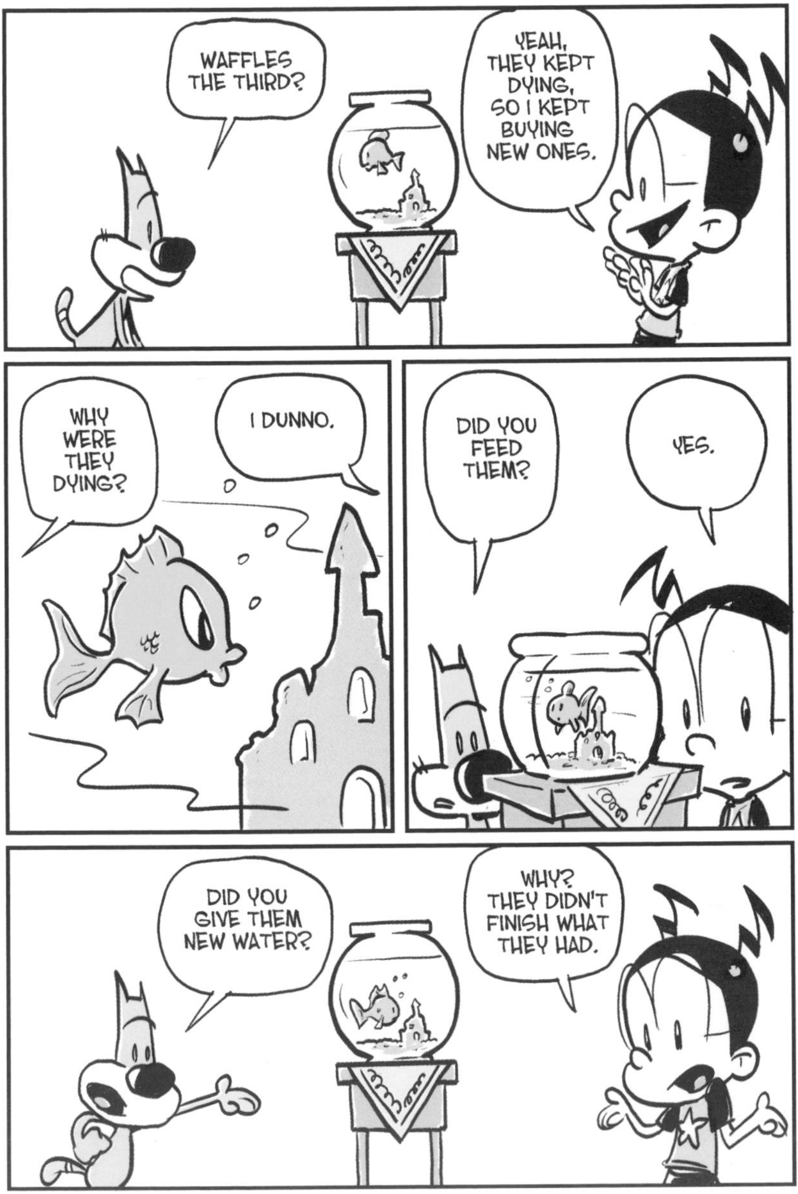
WAFFLES THE THIRD?
YEAH, THEY KEPT DYING, SO I KEPT BUYING NEW ONES.
WHY WERE THEY DYING?
I DUNNO.
DID YOU FEED THEM?
YES.
DID YOU GIVE THEM NEW WATER?
WHY? THEY DIDN'T FINISH WHAT THEY HAD.

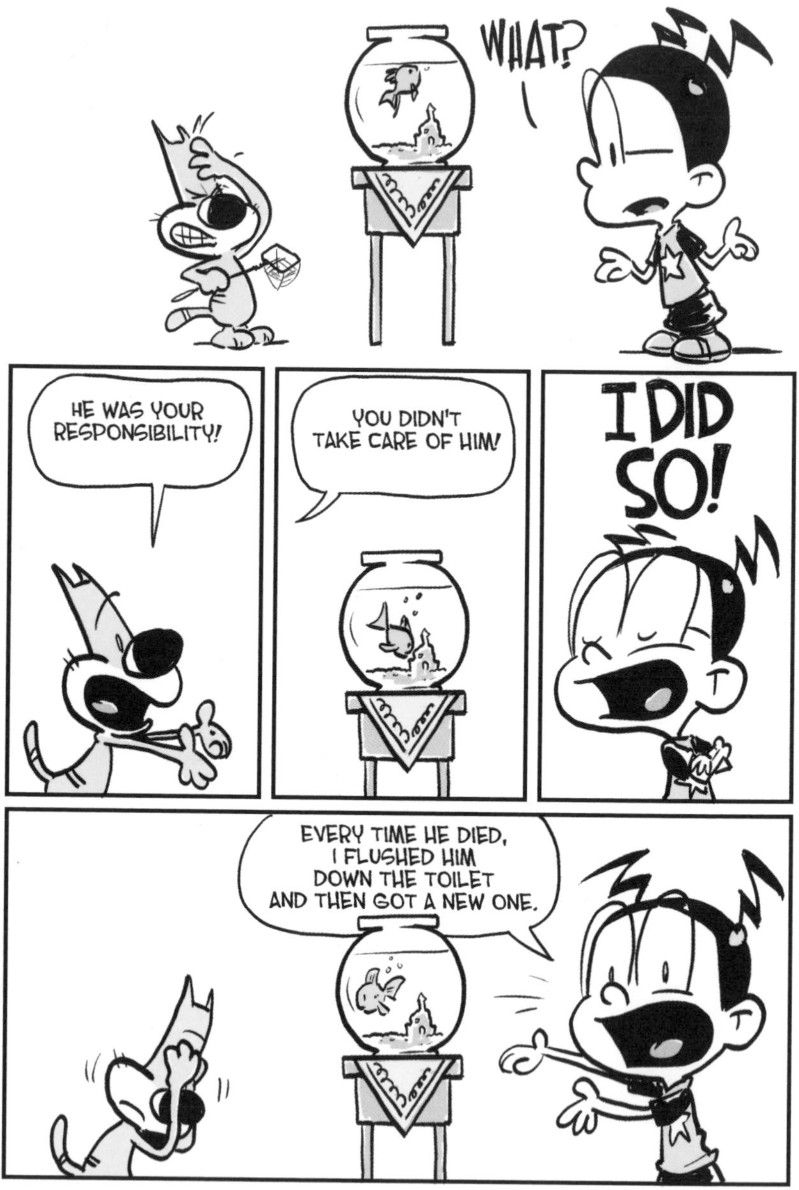
WHAT?
HE WAS YOUR RESPONSIBILITY!
YOU DIDN'T TAKE CARE OF HIM!
I DID SO!
EVERY TIME HE DIED, I FLUSHED HIM DOWN THE TOILET AND THEN GOT A NEW ONE.

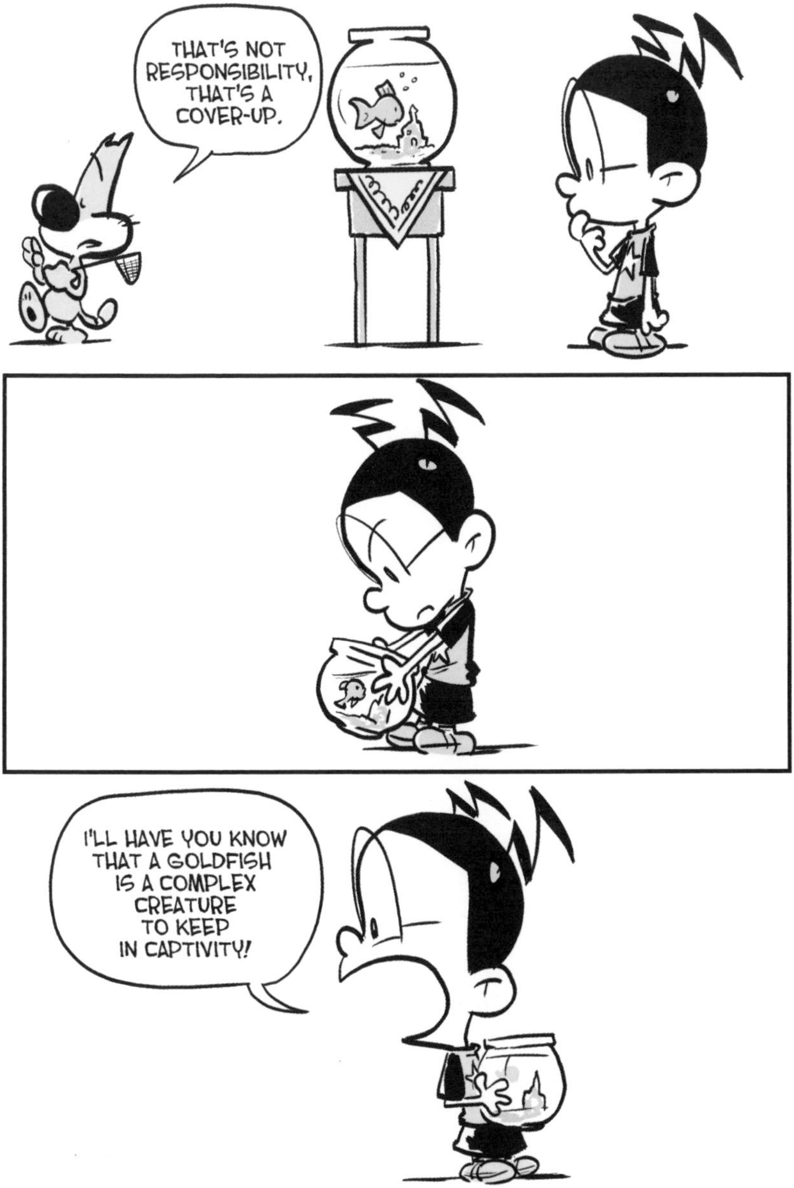
THAT'S NOT RESPONSIBILITY, THAT'S A COVER-UP.
I'LL HAVE YOU KNOW THAT A GOLDFISH IS A COMPLEX CREATURE TO KEEP IN CAPTIVITY!

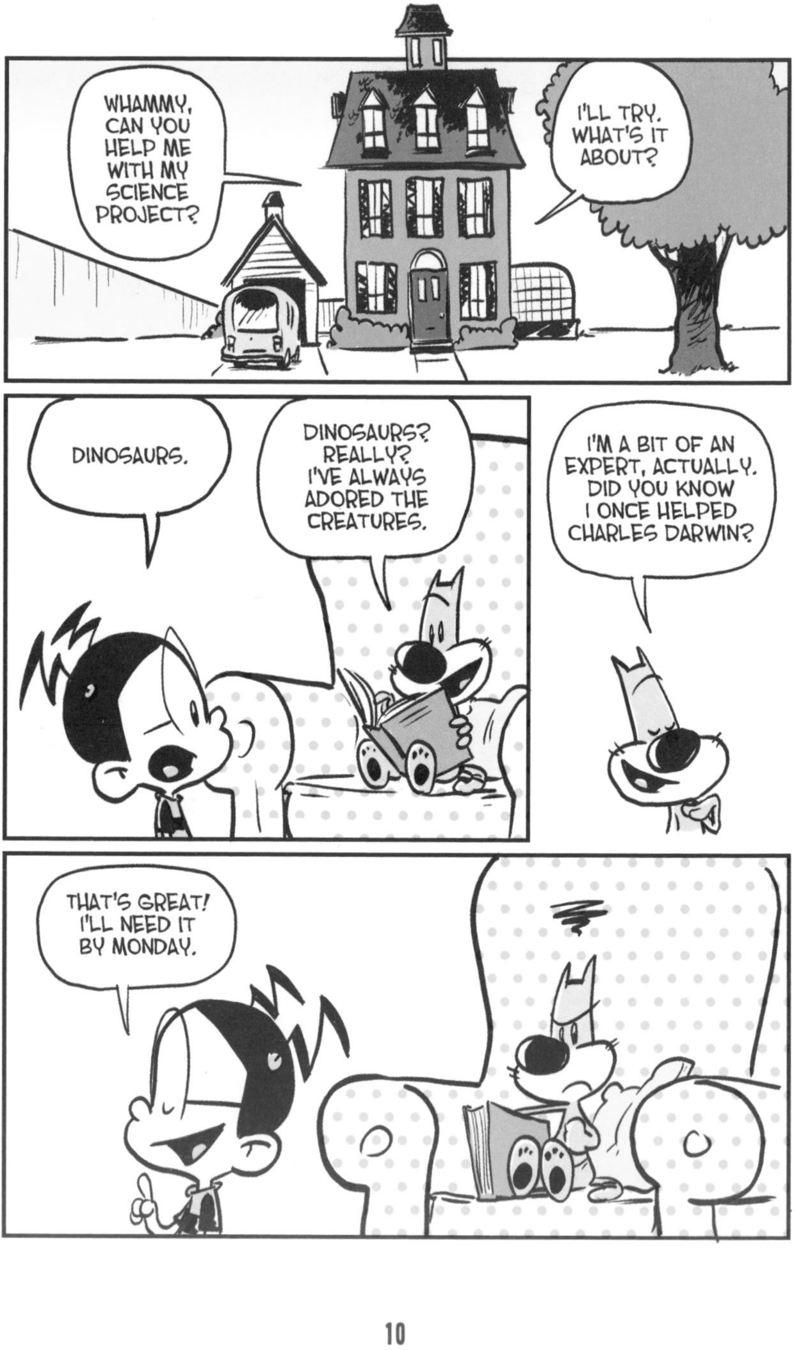
WHAMMY, CAN YOU HELP ME WITH MY SCIENCE PROJECT?
I'LL TRY. WHAT'S IT ABOUT?
DINOSAURS.
DINOSAURS? REALLY? I'VE ALWAYS ADORED THE CREATURES.
I'M A BIT OF AN EXPERT, ACTUALLY. DID YOU KNOW I ONCE HELPED CHARLES DARWIN?
THAT'S GREAT! I'LL NEED IT BY MONDAY.

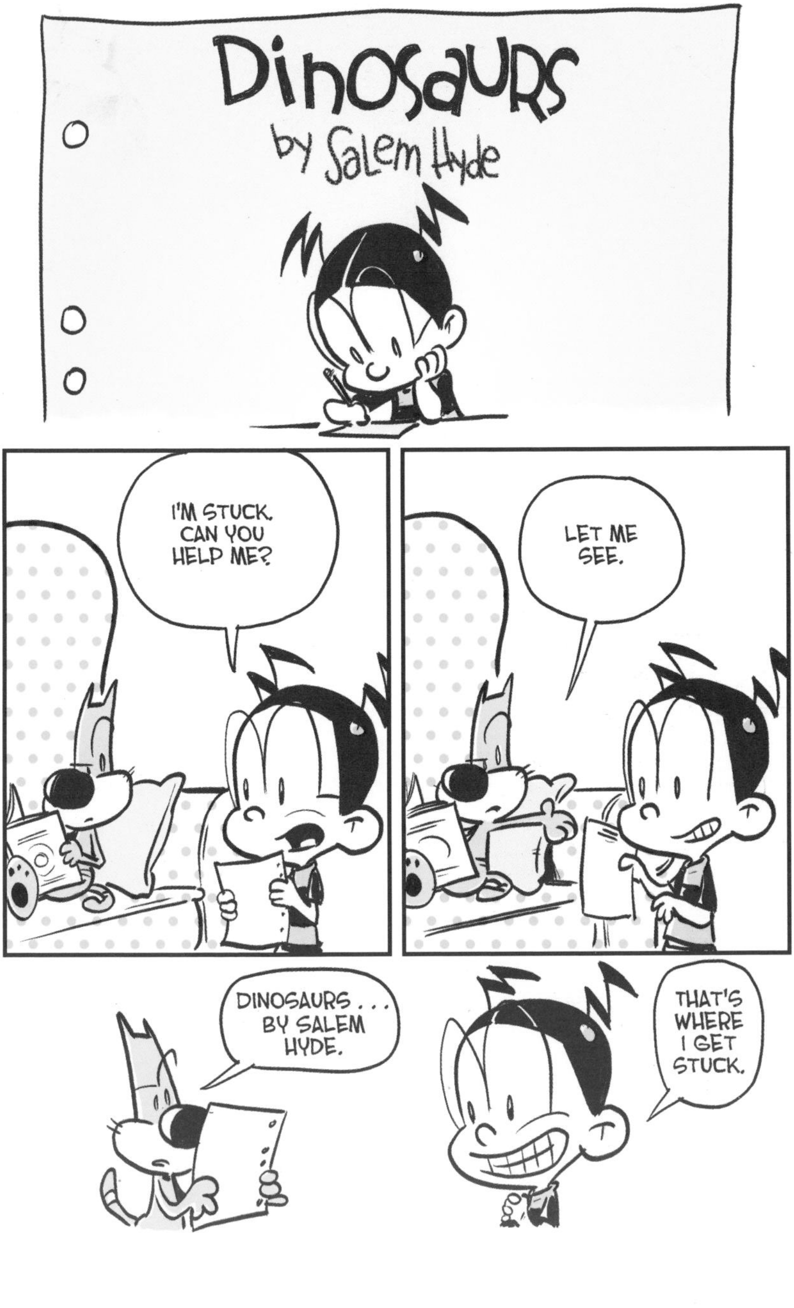
Dinosaurs
by Salem Hyde
I'M STUCK. CAN YOU HELP ME?
LET ME SEE.
DINOSAURS . . . BY SALEM HYDE.
THAT'S WHERE I GET STUCK.

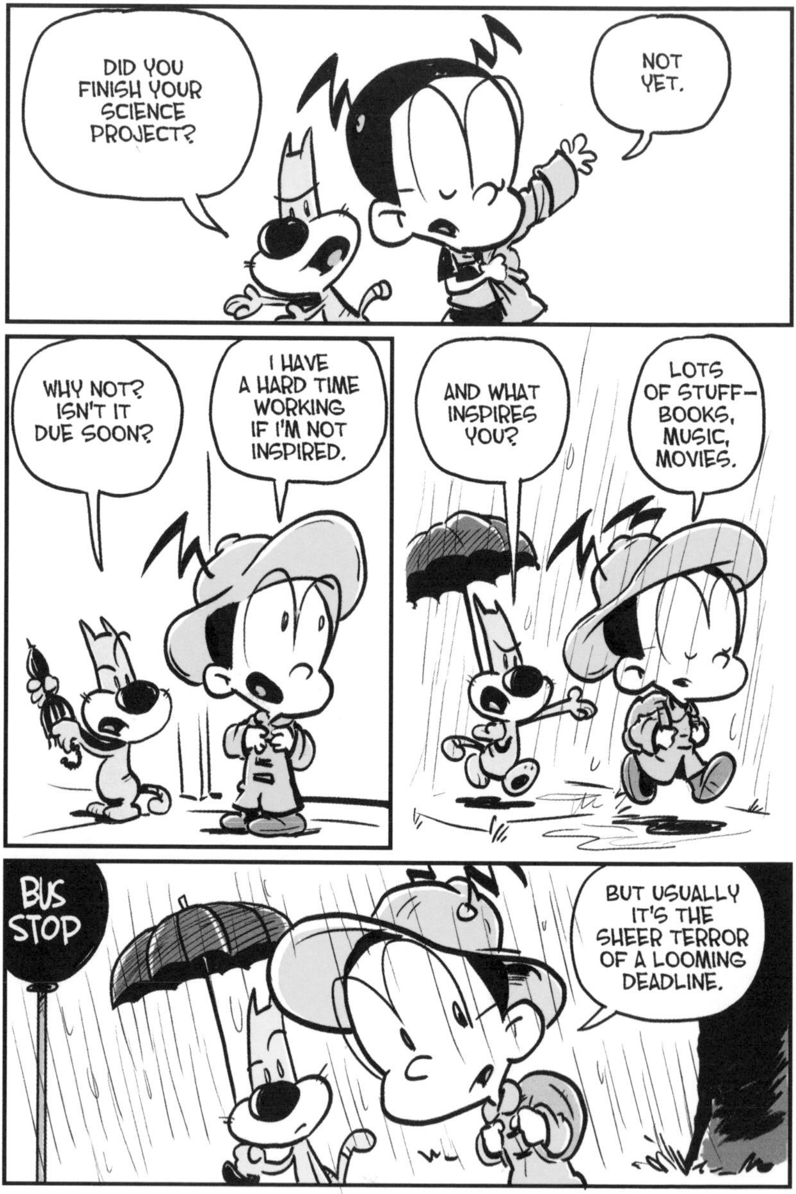
DID YOU FINISH YOUR SCIENCE PROJECT?
NOT YET.
WHY NOT? ISN'T IT DUE SOON?
I HAVE A HARD TIME WORKING IF I'M NOT INSPIRED.
AND WHAT INSPIRES YOU?
LOTS OF STUFF— BOOKS, MUSIC, MOVIES.
BUS STOP
BUT USUALLY IT'S THE SHEER TERROR OF A LOOMING DEADLINE.

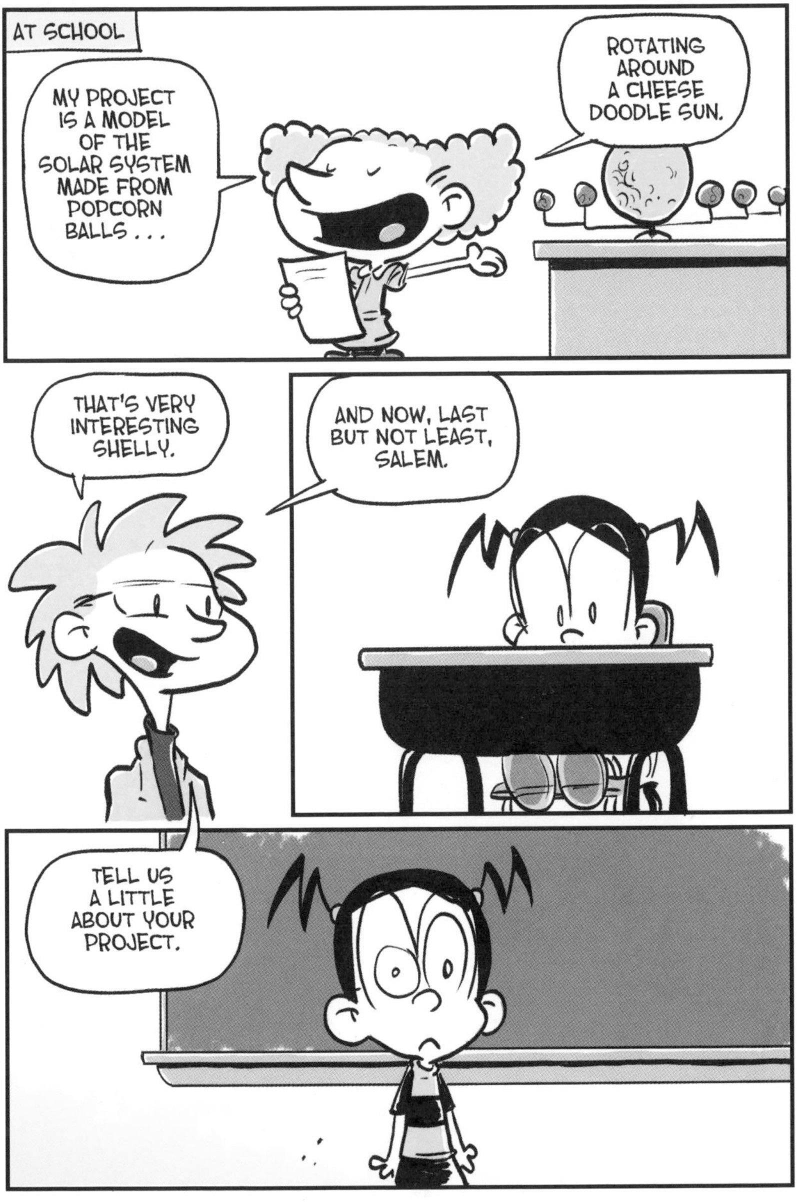
AT SCHOOL
MY PROJECT IS A MODEL OF THE SOLAR SYSTEM MADE FROM POPCORN BALLS . . .
ROTATING AROUND A CHEESE DOODLE SUN.
THAT'S VERY INTERESTING SHELLY.
AND NOW, LAST BUT NOT LEAST, SALEM.
TELL US A LITTLE ABOUT YOUR PROJECT.

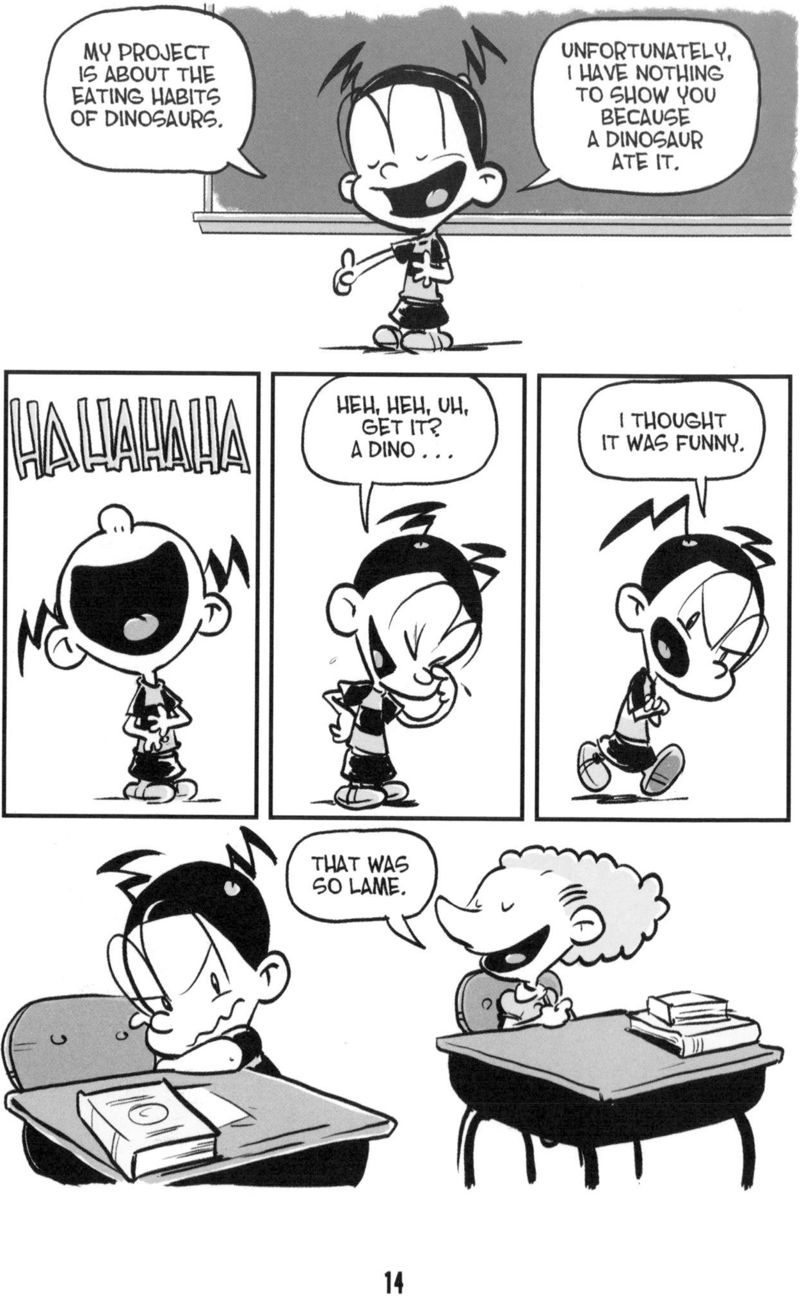
MY PROJECT IS ABOUT THE EATING HABITS OF DINOSAURS.
UNFORTUNATELY, I HAVE NOTHING TO SHOW YOU BECAUSE A DINOSAUR ATE IT.
HA HA HA HA HA
HEH, HEH, UH, GET IT? A DINO . . .
I THOUGHT IT WAS FUNNY.
THAT WAS SO LAME.

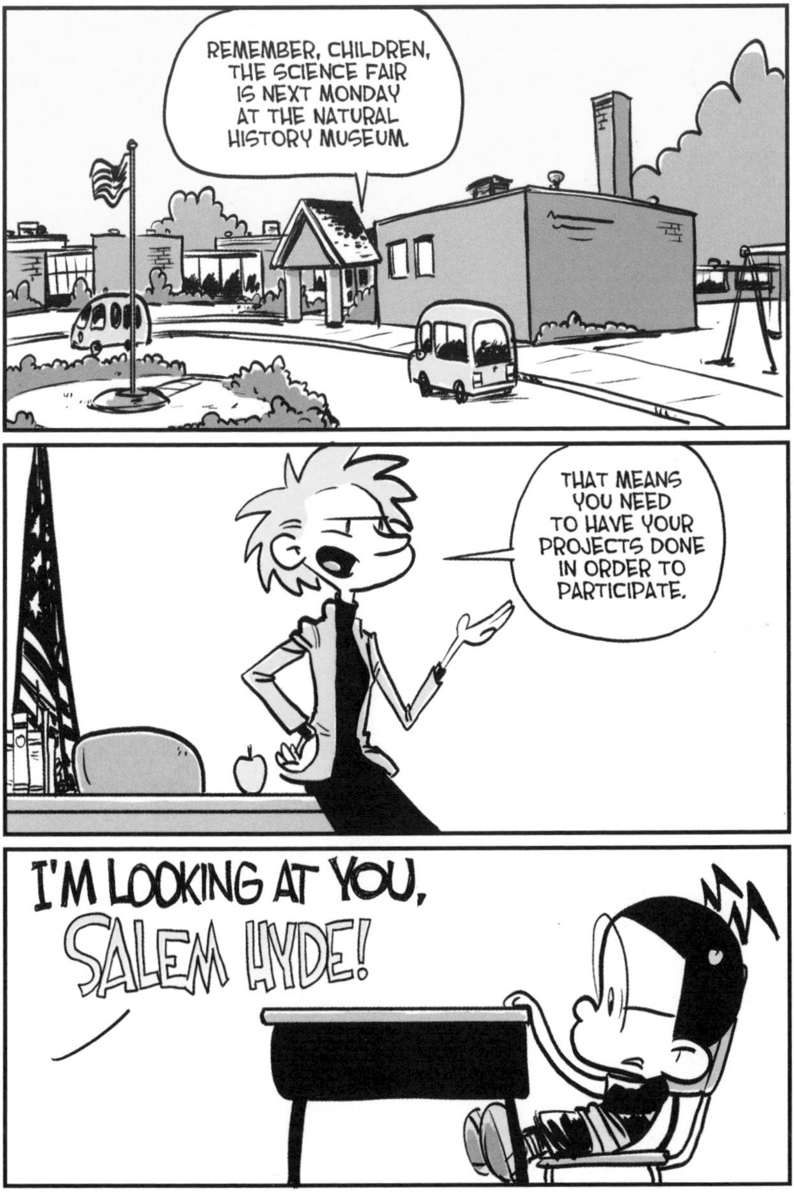
REMEMBER, CHILDREN, THE SCIENCE FAIR IS NEXT MONDAY AT THE NATURAL HISTORY MUSEUM.
THAT MEANS YOU NEED TO HAVE YOUR PROJECTS DONE IN ORDER TO PARTICIPATE.
I'M LOOKING AT YOU, SALEM HYDE!

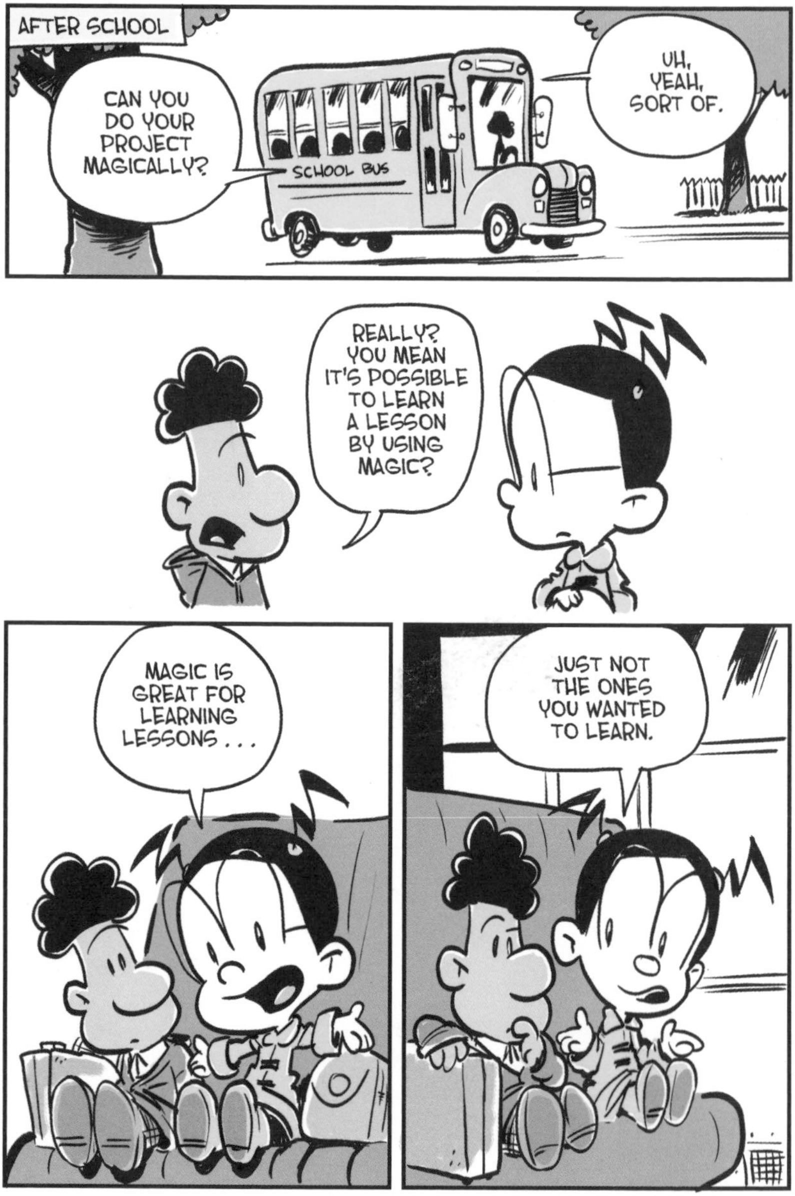
AFTER SCHOOL
CAN YOU DO YOUR PROJECT MAGICALLY?
SCHOOL BUS
UH, YEAH, SORT OF.
REALLY? YOU MEAN IT'S POSSIBLE TO LEARN A LESSON BY USING MAGIC?
MAGIC IS GREAT FOR LEARNING LESSONS . . .
JUST NOT THE ONES YOU WANTED TO LEARN.

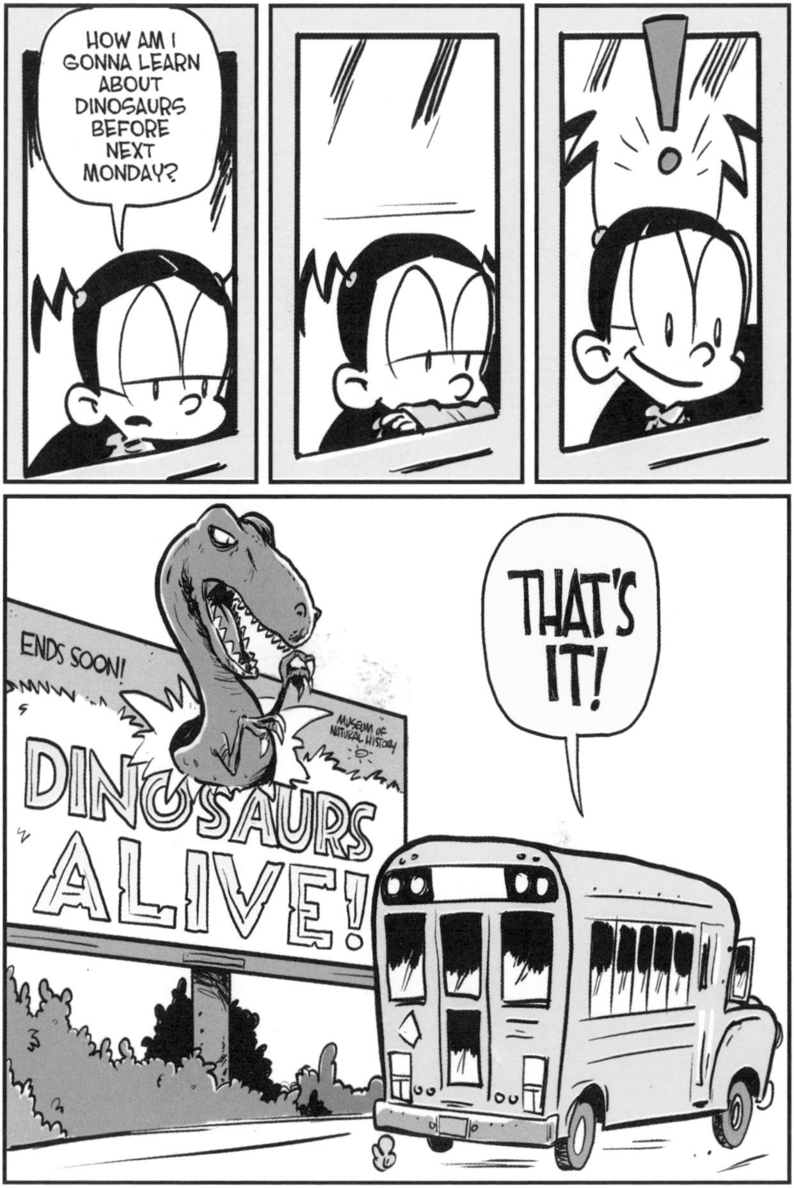
HOW AM I GONNA LEARN ABOUT DINOSAURS BEFORE NEXT MONDAY?
ENDS SOON!
MUSEUM OF NATURAL HISTORY
DINOSAURS ALIVE!
THAT'S IT!

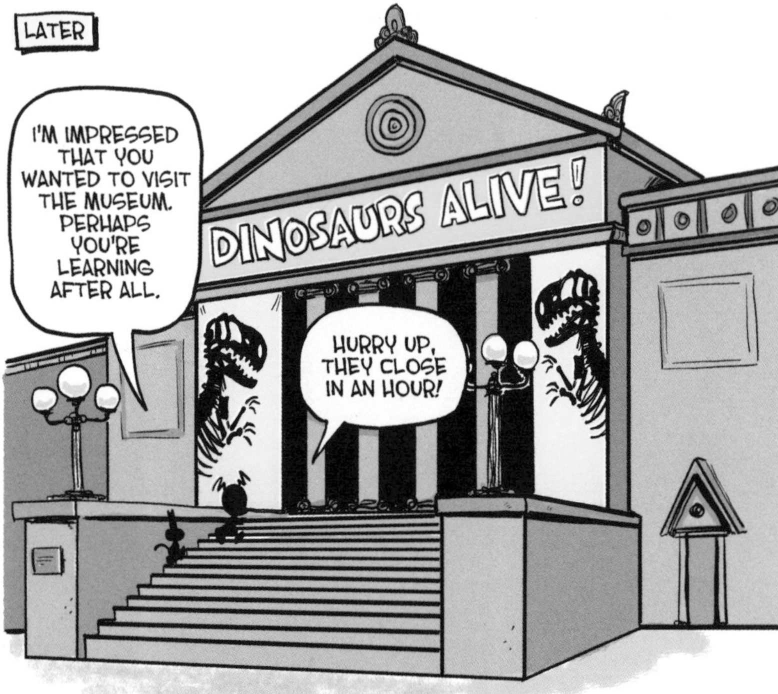
LATER
I'M IMPRESSED THAT YOU WANTED TO VISIT THE MUSEUM. PERHAPS YOU'RE LEARNING AFTER ALL.
DINOSAURS ALIVE!
HURRY UP, THEY CLOSE IN AN HOUR!

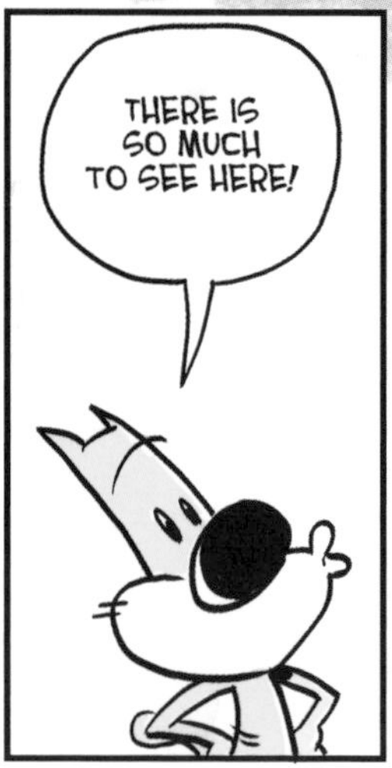
THERE IS SO MUCH TO SEE HERE!

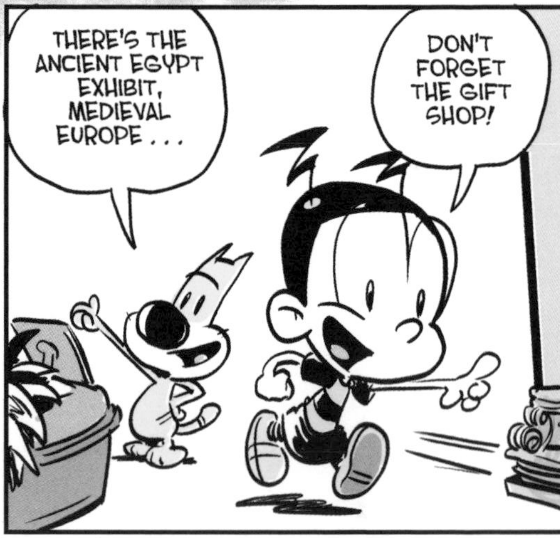
THERE'S THE ANCIENT EGYPT EXHIBIT, MEDIEVAL EUROPE . . .
DON'T FORGET THE GIFT SHOP!

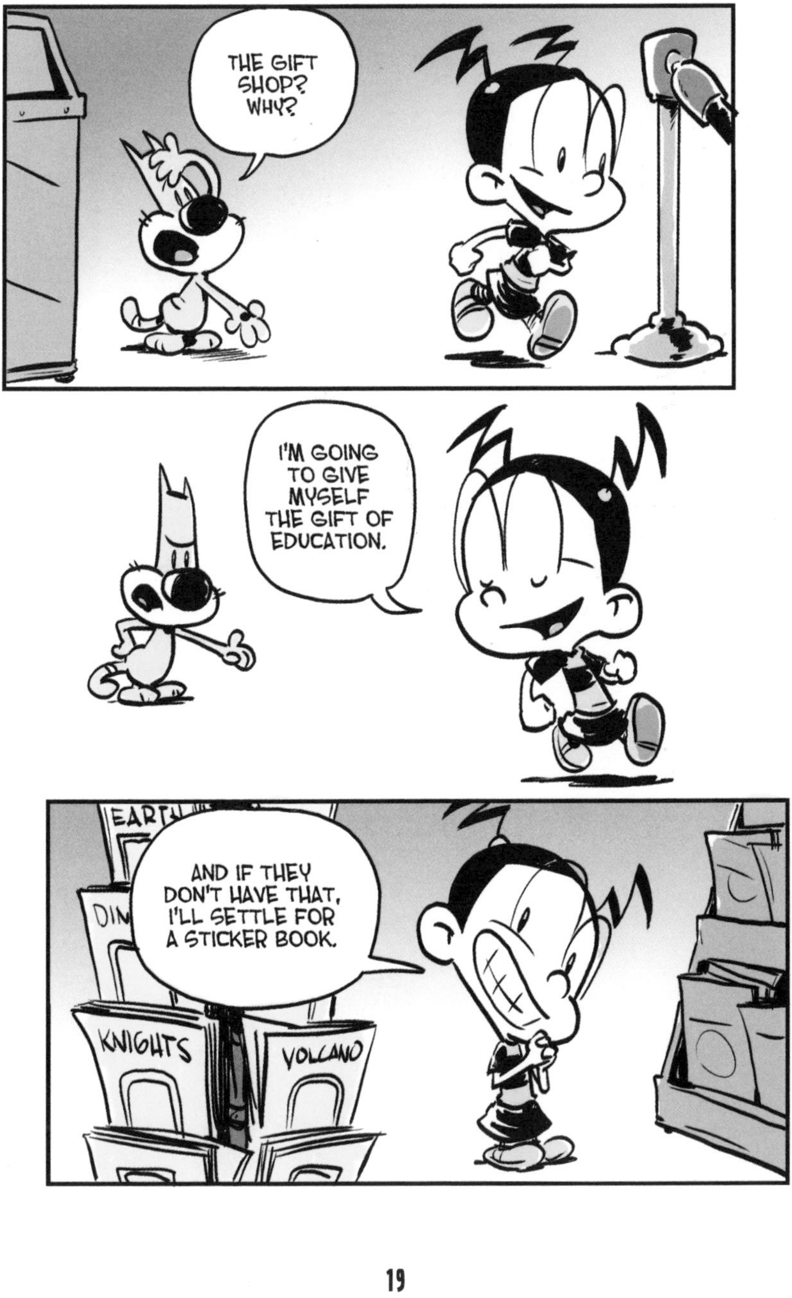

THE GIFT SHOP? WHY?
I'M GOING TO GIVE MYSELF THE GIFT OF EDUCATION.
AND IF THEY DON'T HAVE THAT, I'LL SETTLE FOR A STICKER BOOK.
KNIGHTS
VOLCANO

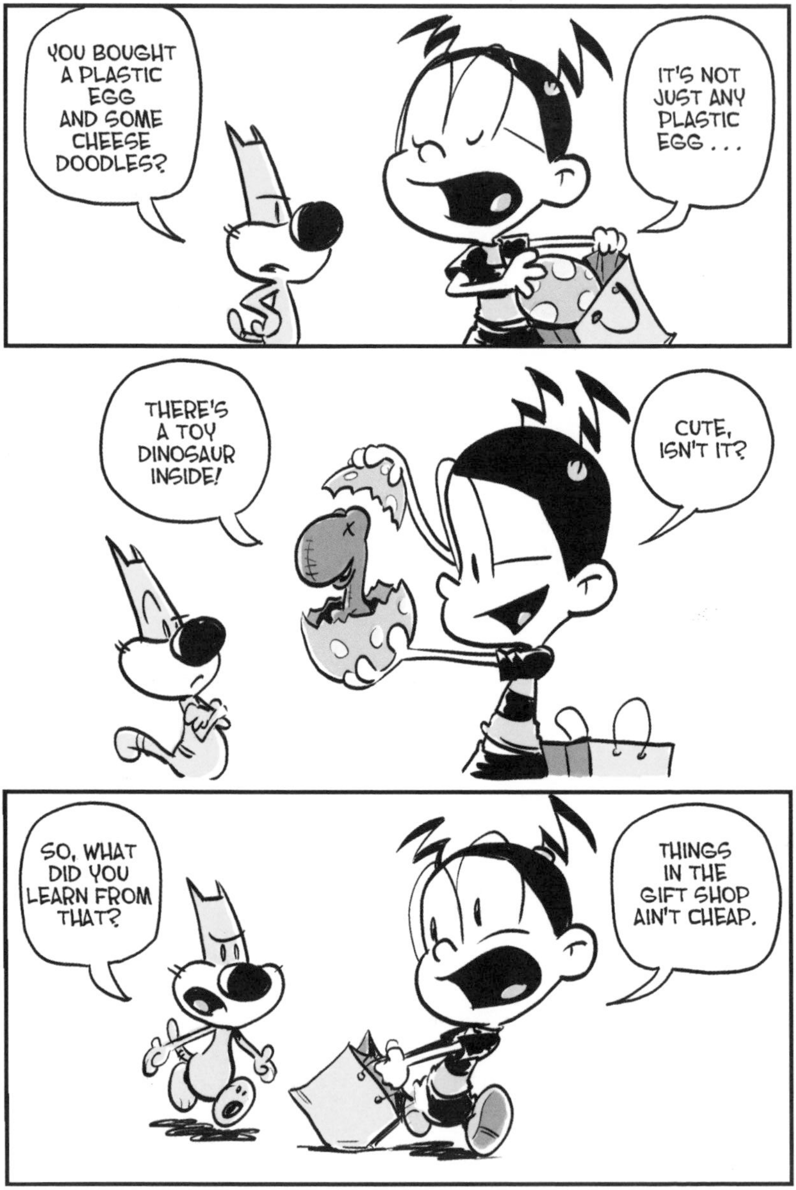
YOU BOUGHT A PLASTIC EGG AND SOME CHEESE DOODLES?
IT'S NOT JUST ANY PLASTIC EGG . . .
THERE'S A TOY DINOSAUR INSIDE!
CUTE, ISN'T IT?
SO, WHAT DID YOU LEARN FROM THAT?
THINGS IN THE GIFT SHOP AIN'T CHEAP.

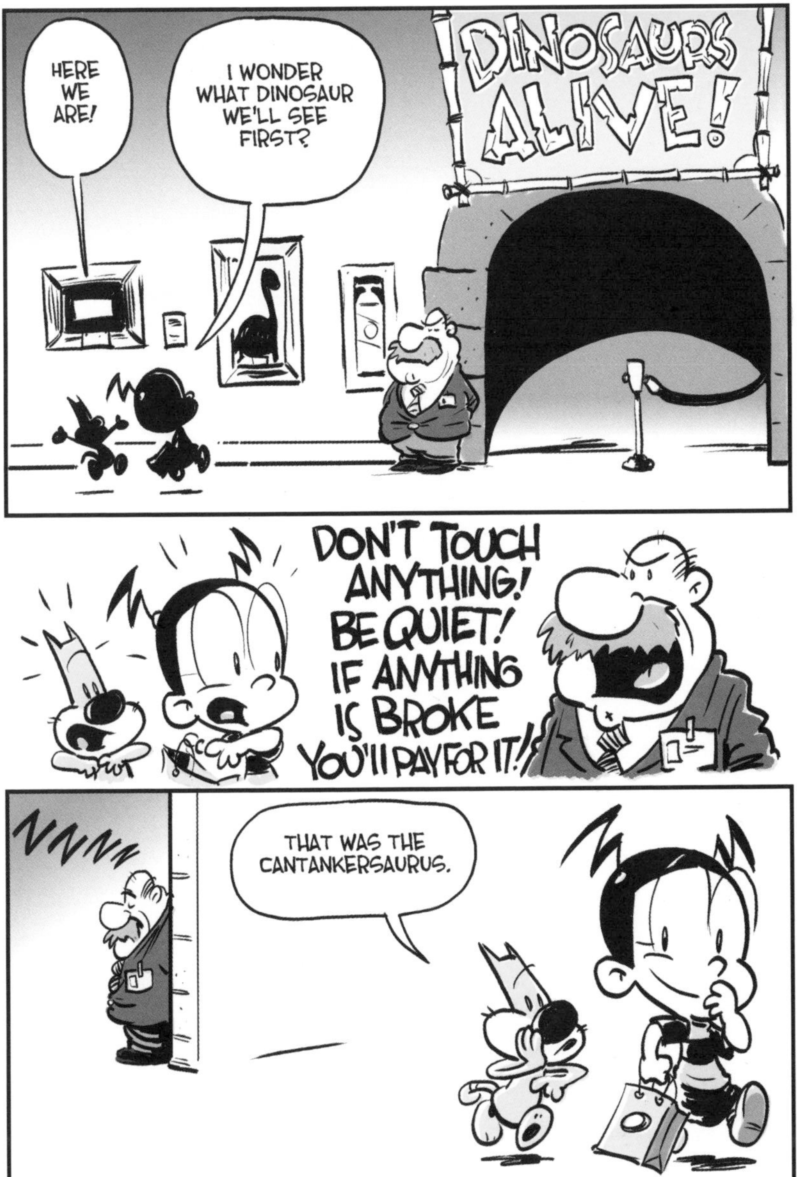
HERE WE ARE!
I WONDER WHAT DINOSAUR WE'LL SEE FIRST?
DINOSAURS ALIVE!
DON'T TOUCH ANYTHING! BE QUIET! IF ANYTHING IS BROKE YOU'll PAY FOR IT!
NNNN
THAT WAS THE CANTANKERSAURUS.

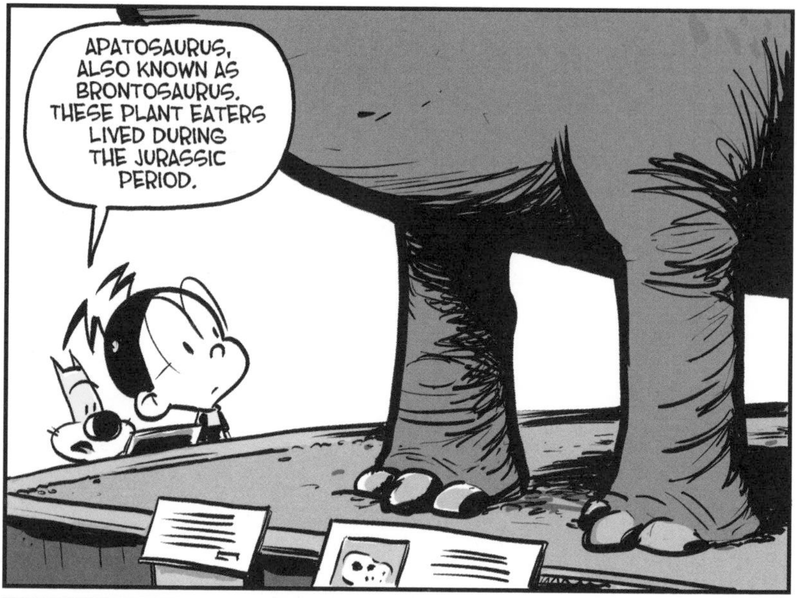
APATOSAURUS, ALSO KNOWN AS BRONTOSAURUS. THESE PLANT EATERS LIVED DURING THE JURASSIC PERIOD.

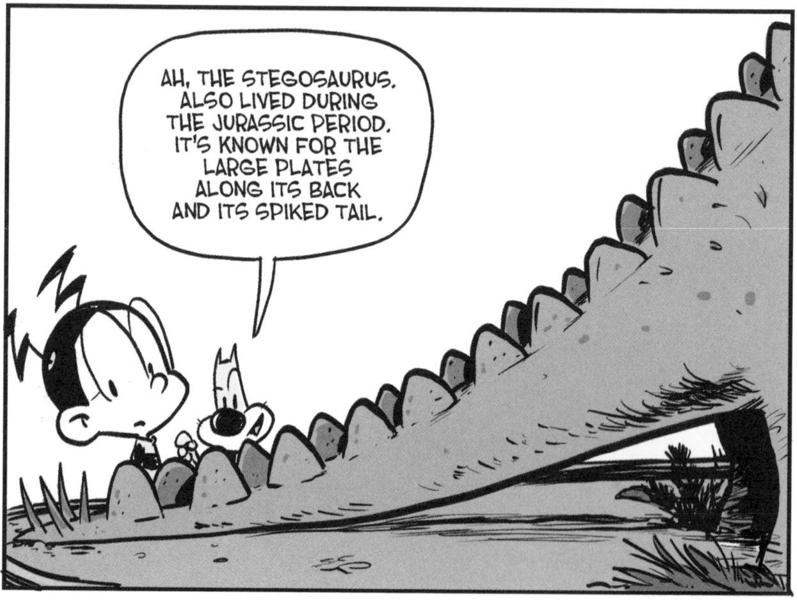
AH, THE STEGOSAURUS. ALSO LIVED DURING THE JURASSIC PERIOD. IT'S KNOWN FOR THE LARGE PLATES ALONG ITS BACK AND ITS SPIKED TAIL.

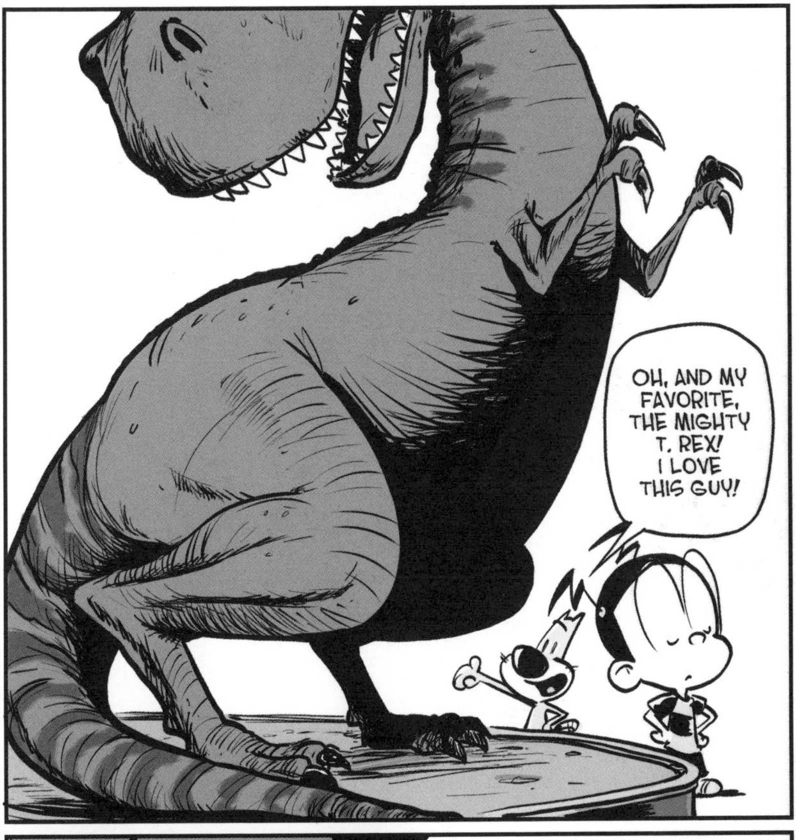
OH, AND MY FAVORITE, THE MIGHTY T. REX! I LOVE THIS GUY!

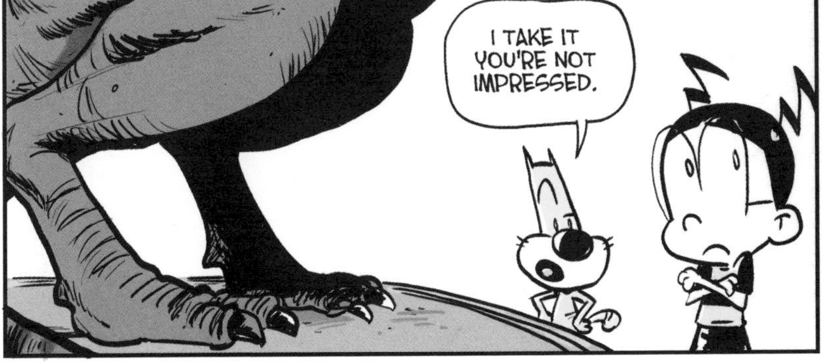
I TAKE IT YOU'RE NOT IMPRESSED.

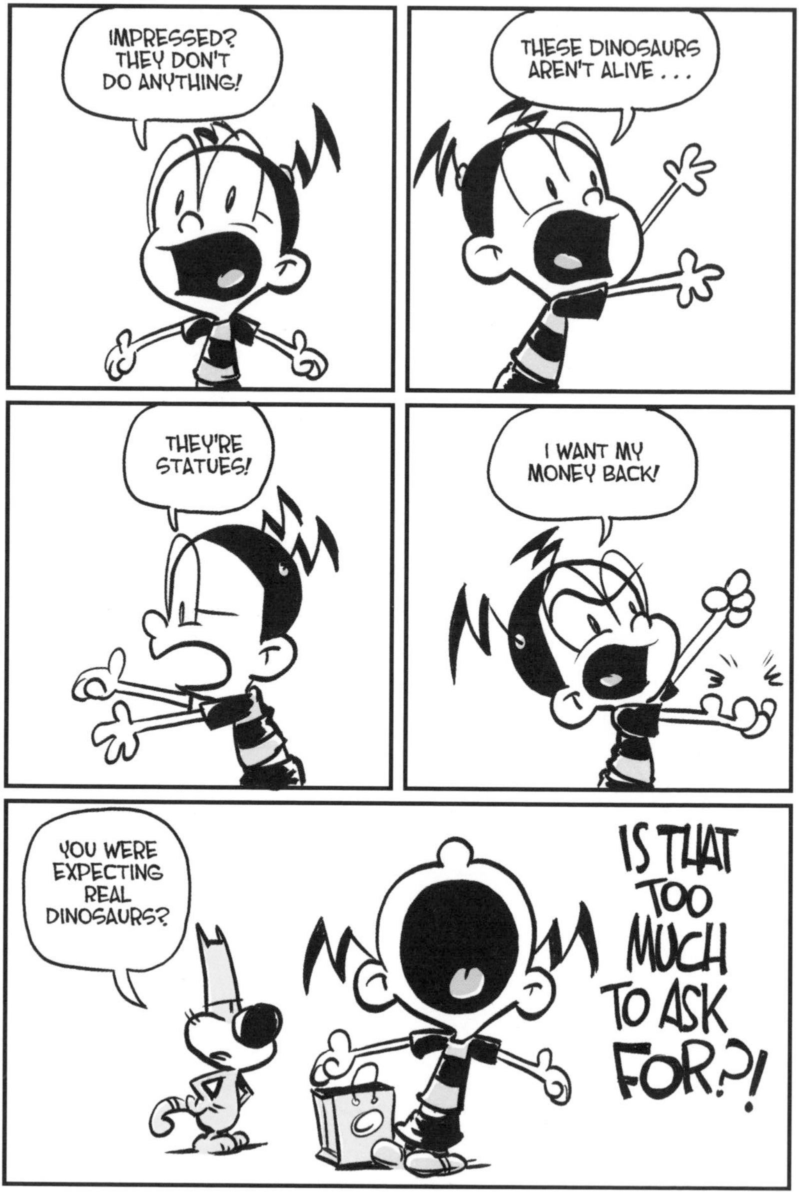
IMPRESSED? THEY DON'T DO ANYTHING!
THESE DINOSAURS AREN'T ALIVE . . .
THEY'RE STATUES!
I WANT MY MONEY BACK!
YOU WERE EXPECTING REAL DINOSAURS?
IS THAT TOO MUCH TO ASK FOR?!

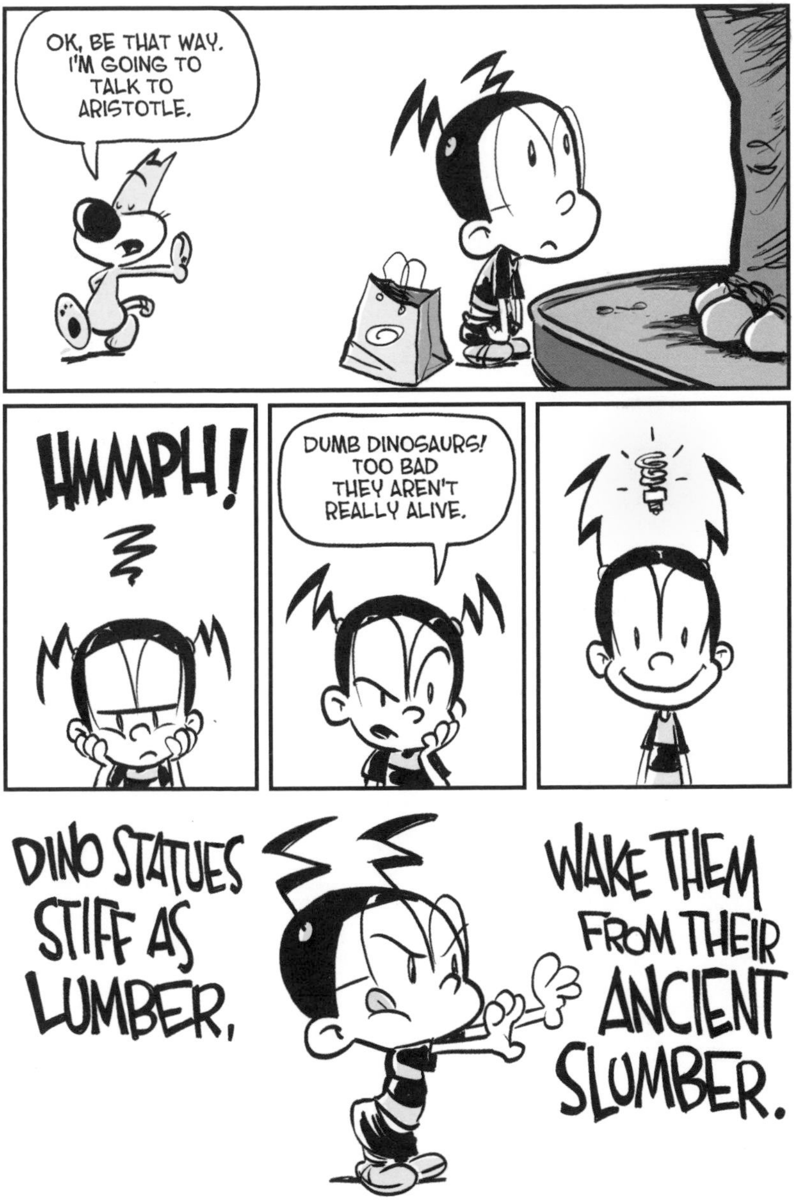
OK, BE THAT WAY. I'M GOING TO TALK TO ARISTOTLE.
HMMPH!
DUMB DINOSAURS! TOO BAD THEY AREN'T REALLY ALIVE.
DINO STATUES STIFF AS LUMBER,
WAKE THEM FROM THEIR ANCIENT SLUMBER.

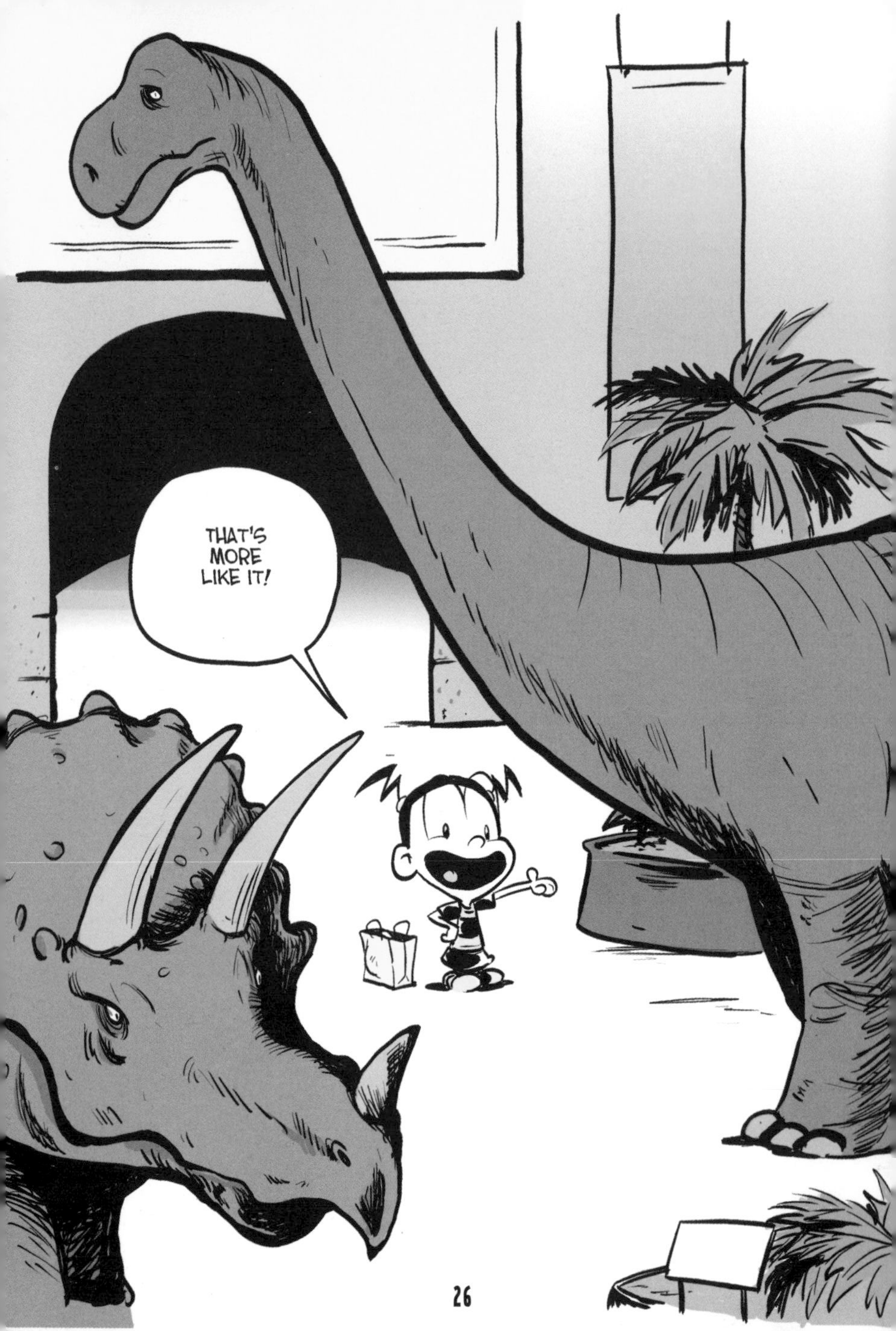
THAT'S MORE LIKE IT!

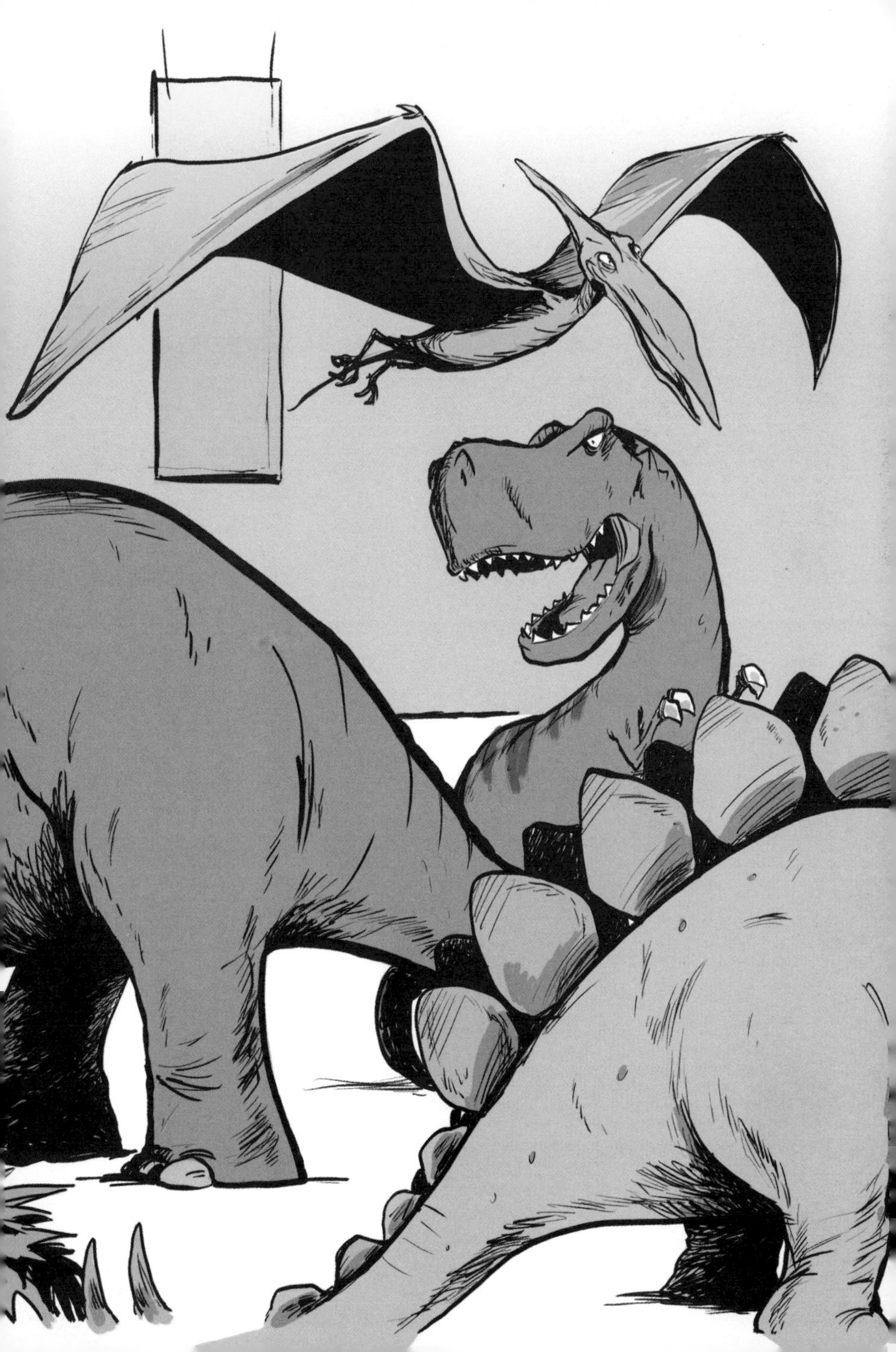

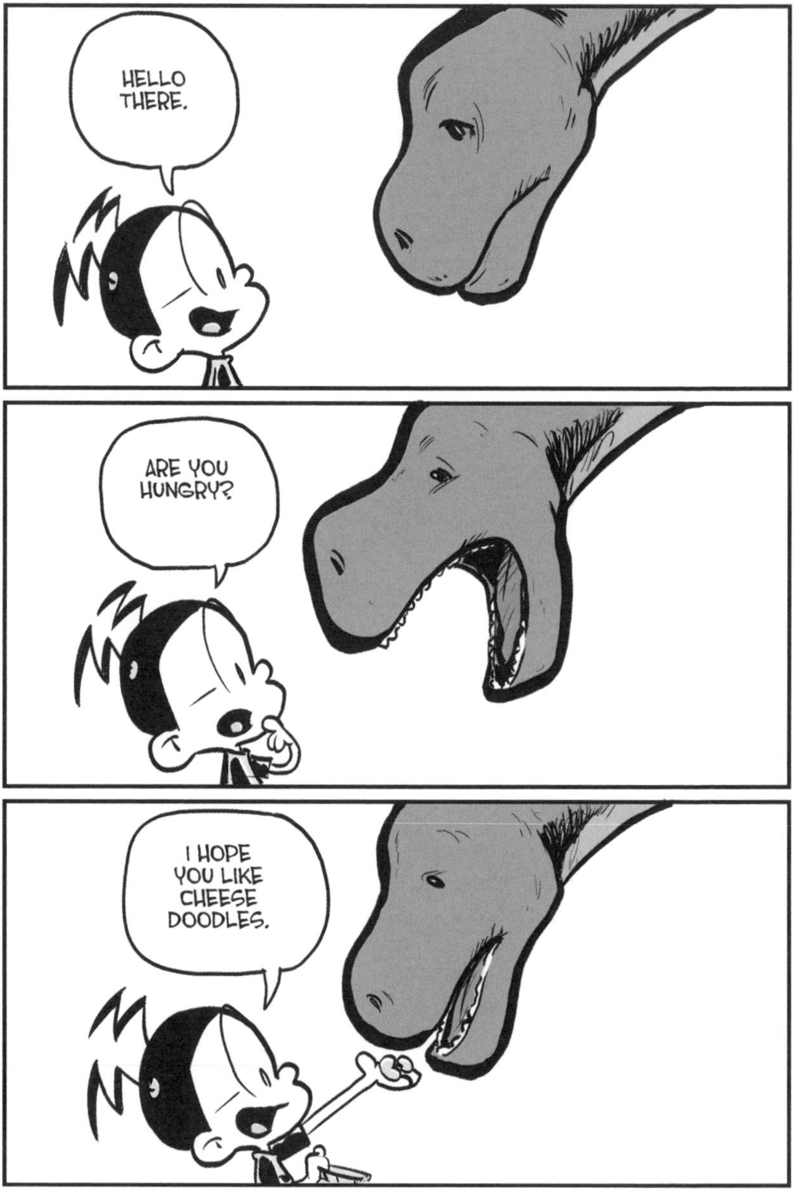
HELLO THERE.
ARE YOU HUNGRY?
I HOPE YOU LIKE CHEESE DOODLES.

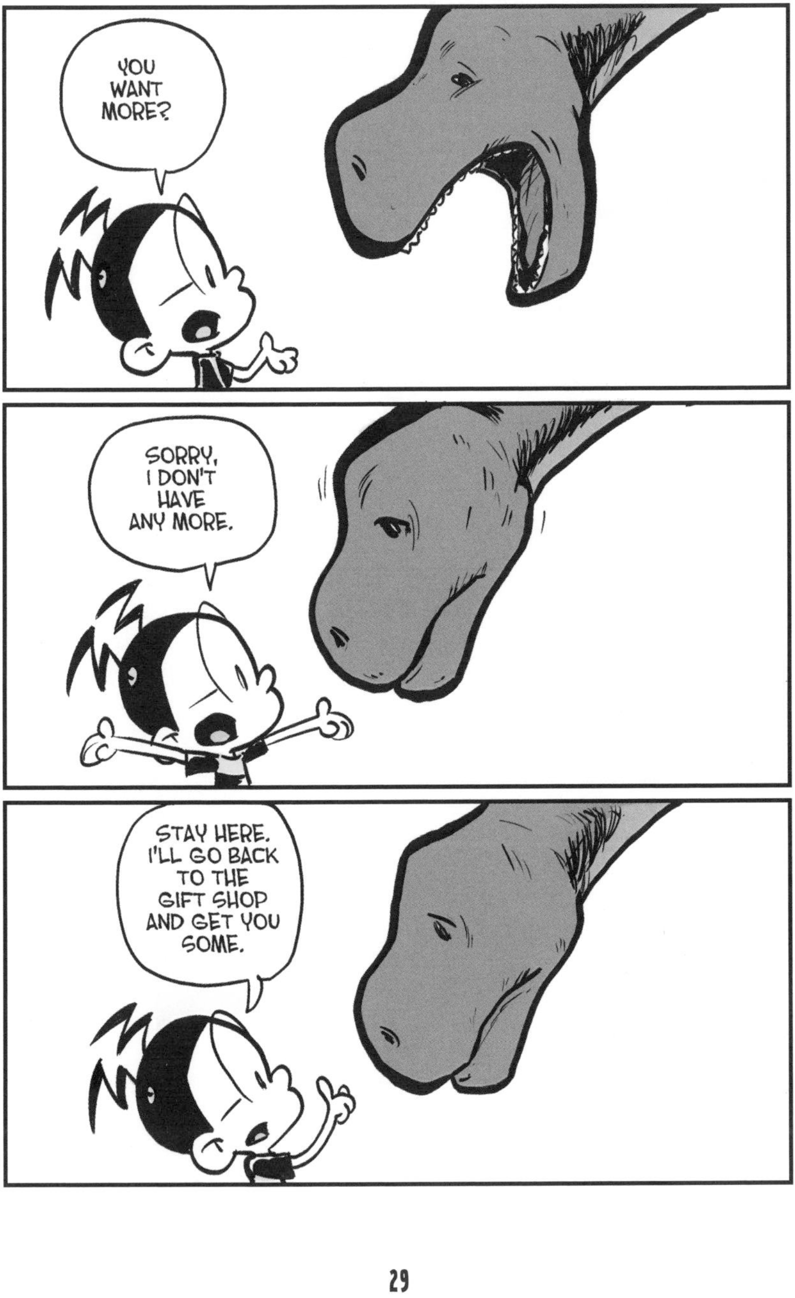
YOU WANT MORE?
SORRY, I DON'T HAVE ANY MORE.
STAY HERE. I'LL GO BACK TO THE GIFT SHOP AND GET YOU SOME.

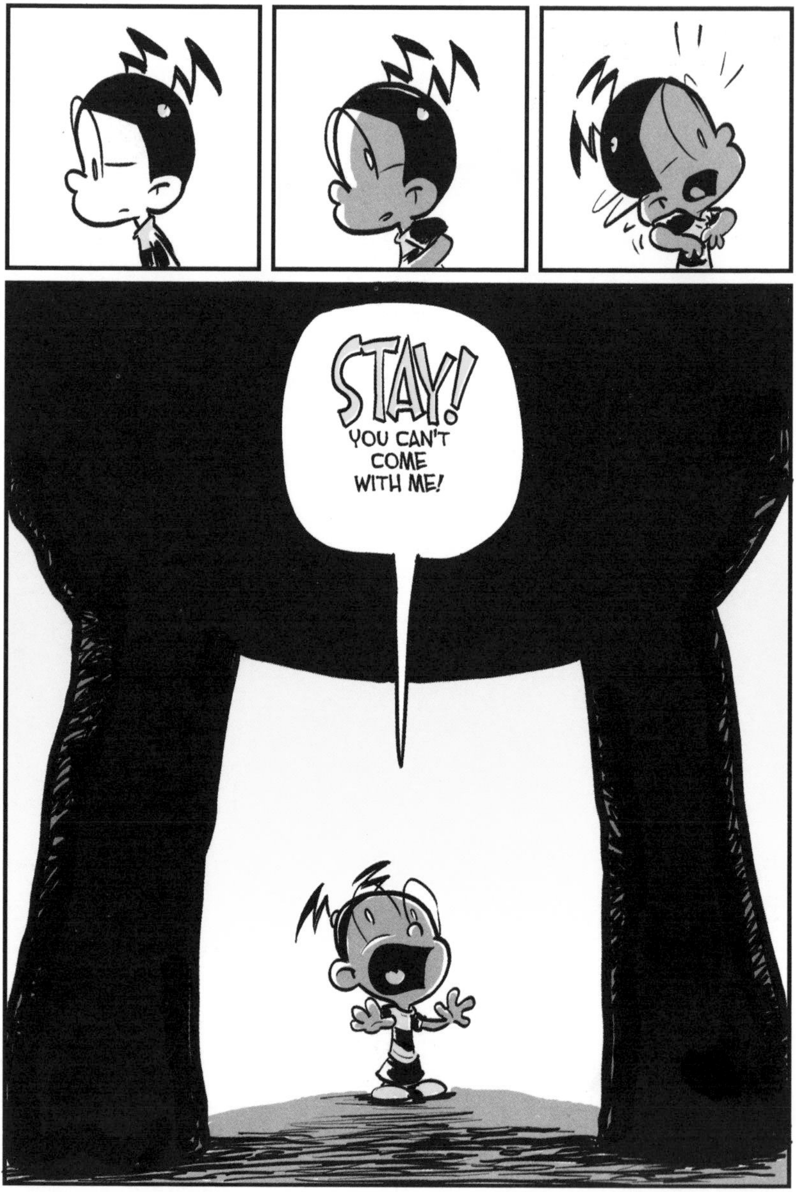
STAY!
YOU CAN'T COME WITH ME!

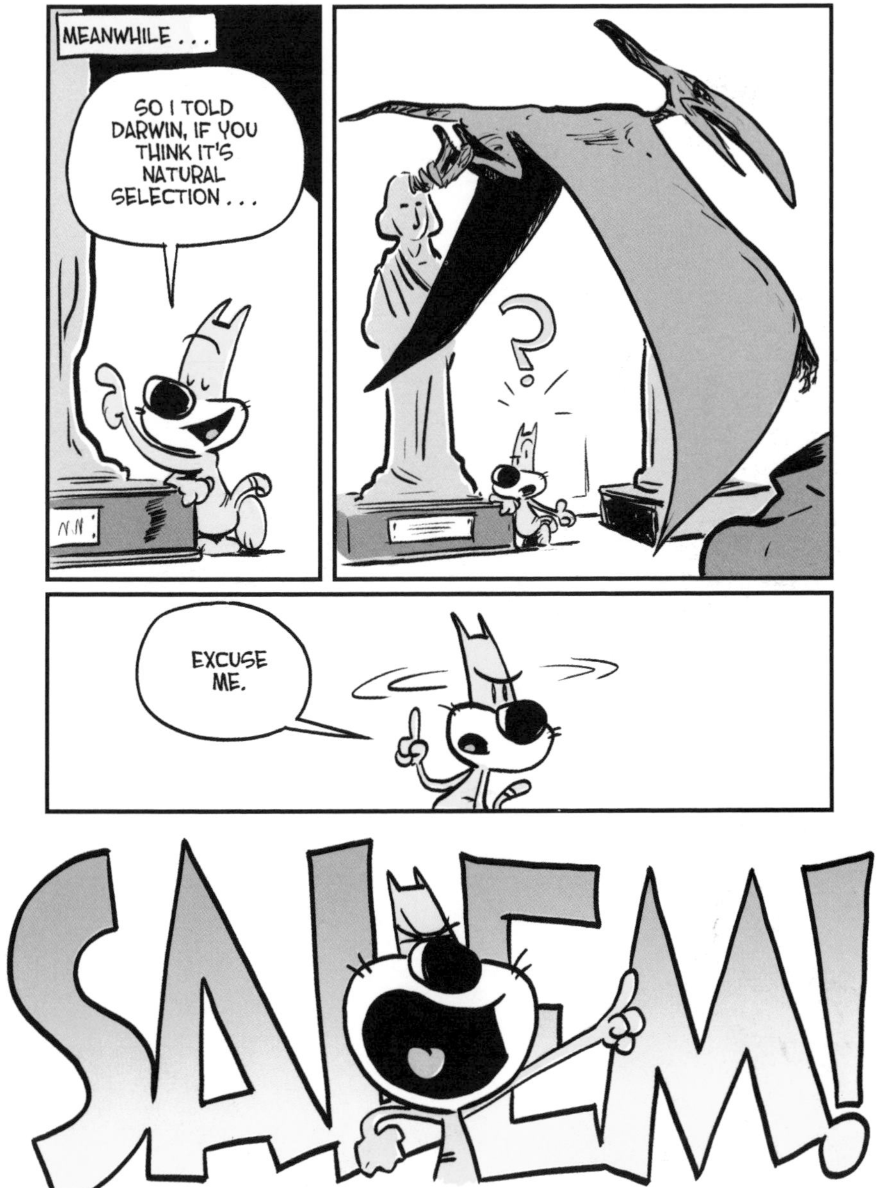

MEANWHILE . . .
SO I TOLD DARWIN, IF YOU THINK IT'S NATURAL SELECTION . . .
?
EXCUSE ME.
SALEM!

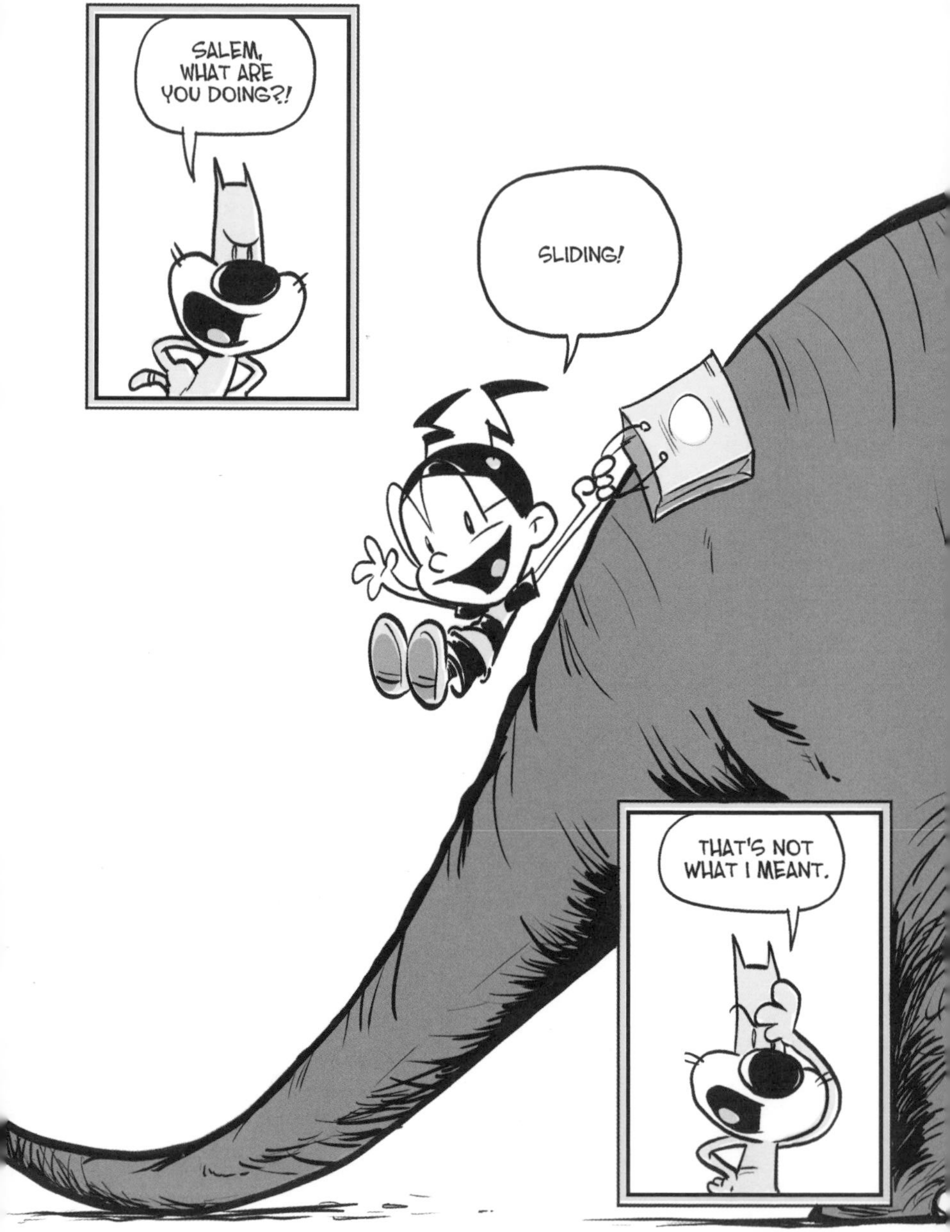
SALEM, WHAT ARE YOU DOING?!
SLIDING!
THAT'S NOT WHAT I MEANT.

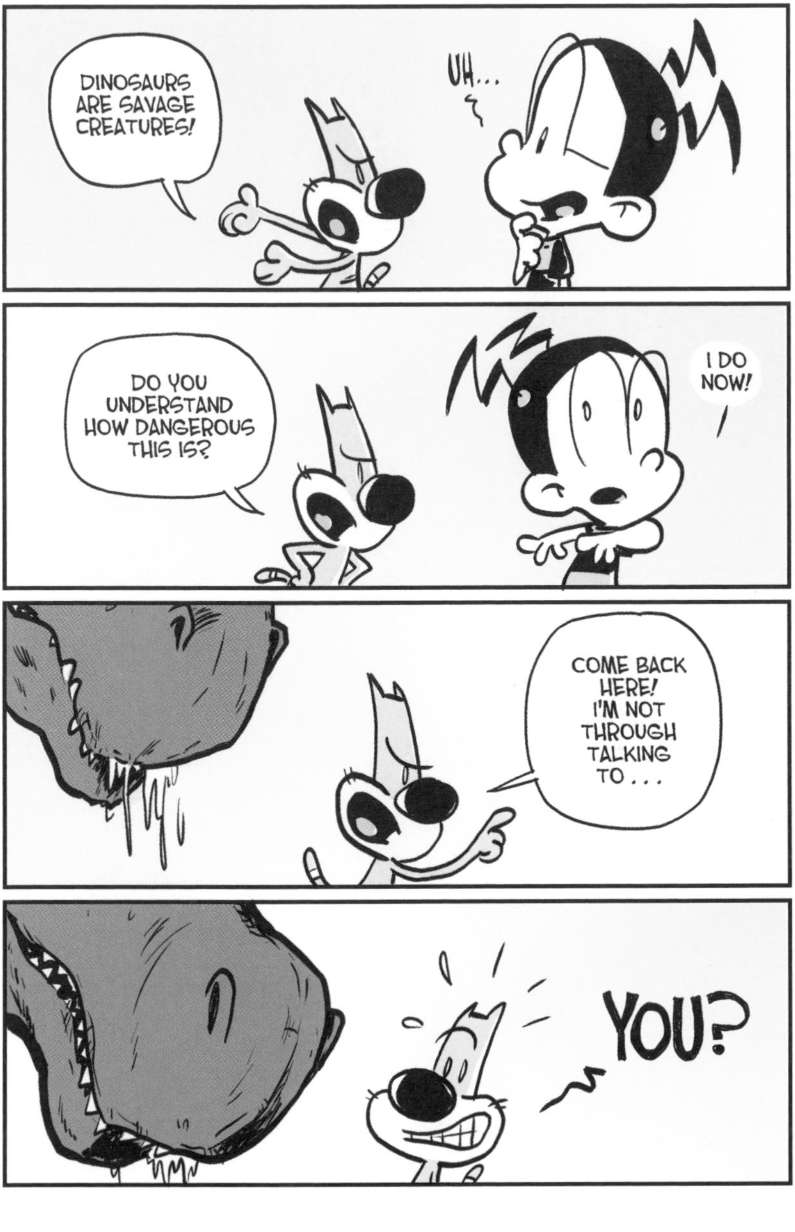
DINOSAURS ARE SAVAGE CREATURES!
UH...
DO YOU UNDERSTAND HOW DANGEROUS THIS IS?
I DO NOW!
COME BACK HERE! I'M NOT THROUGH TALKING TO . . .
YOU?

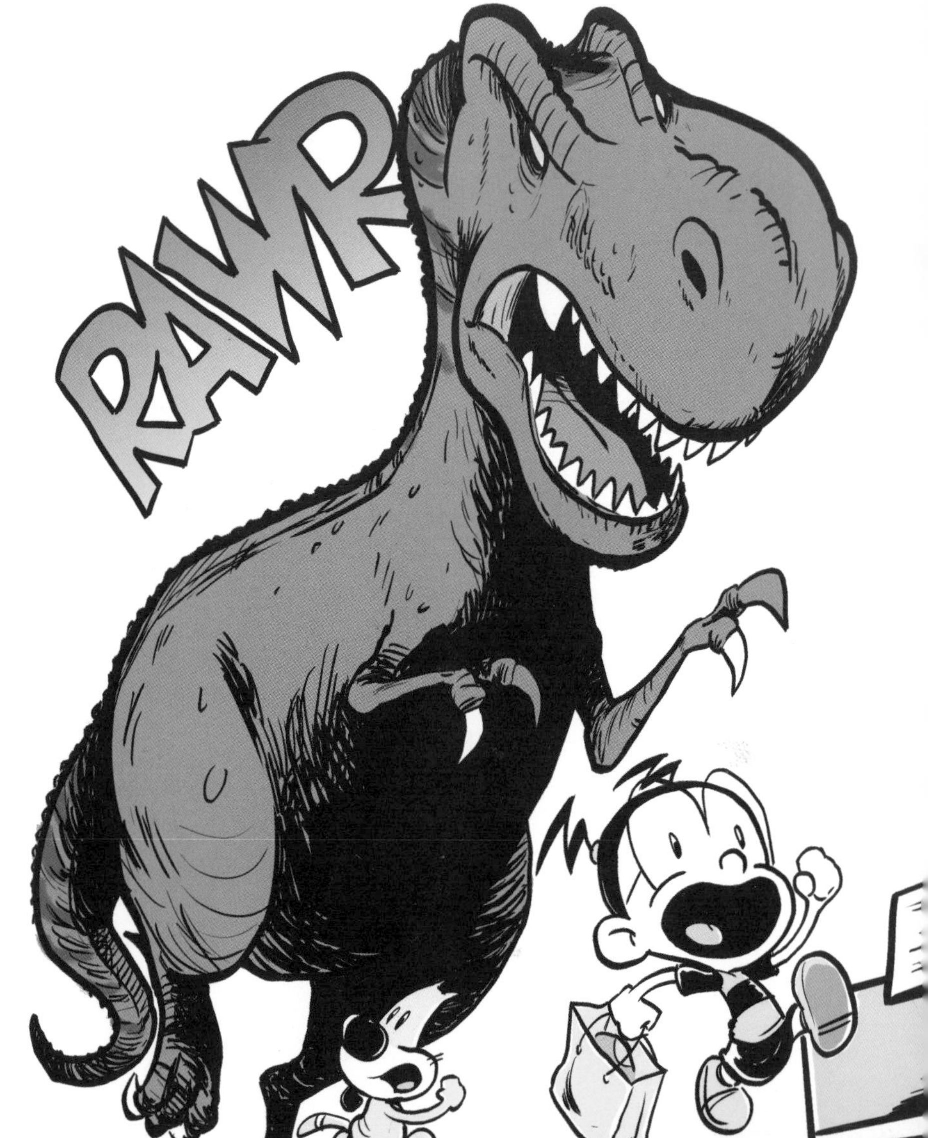
RAWR

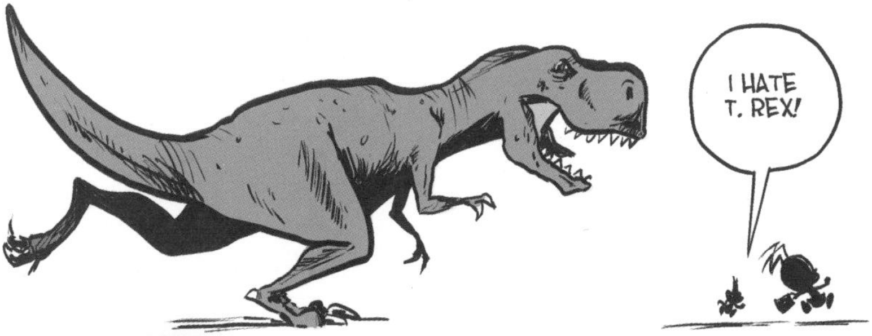
I HATE T. REX!

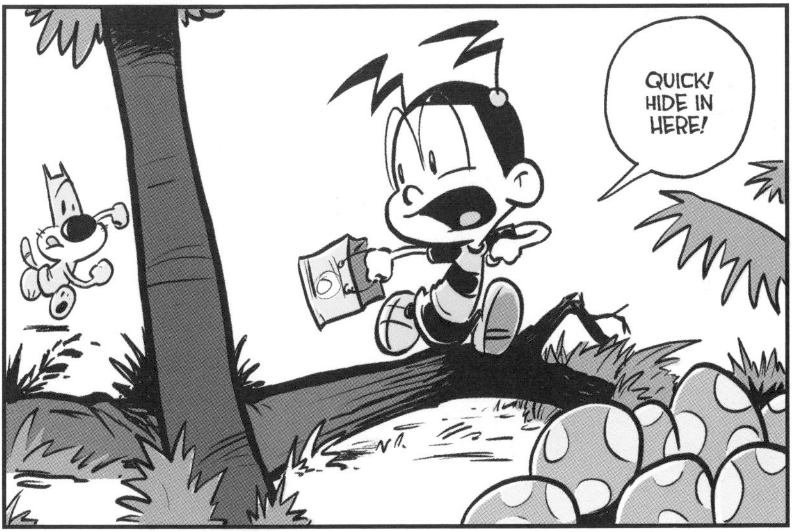
QUICK! HIDE IN HERE!

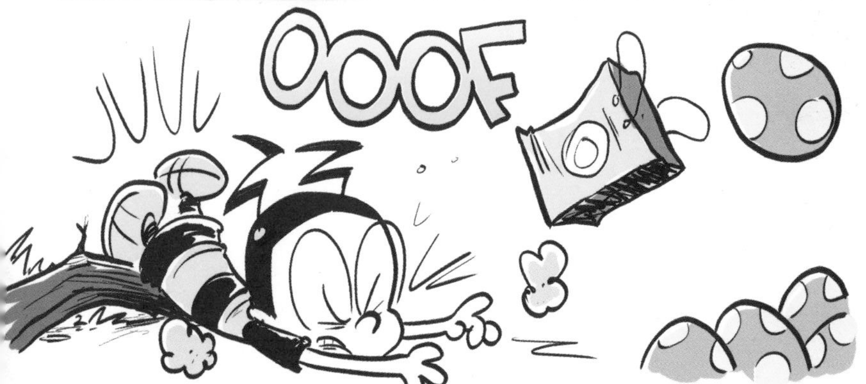
OOOF

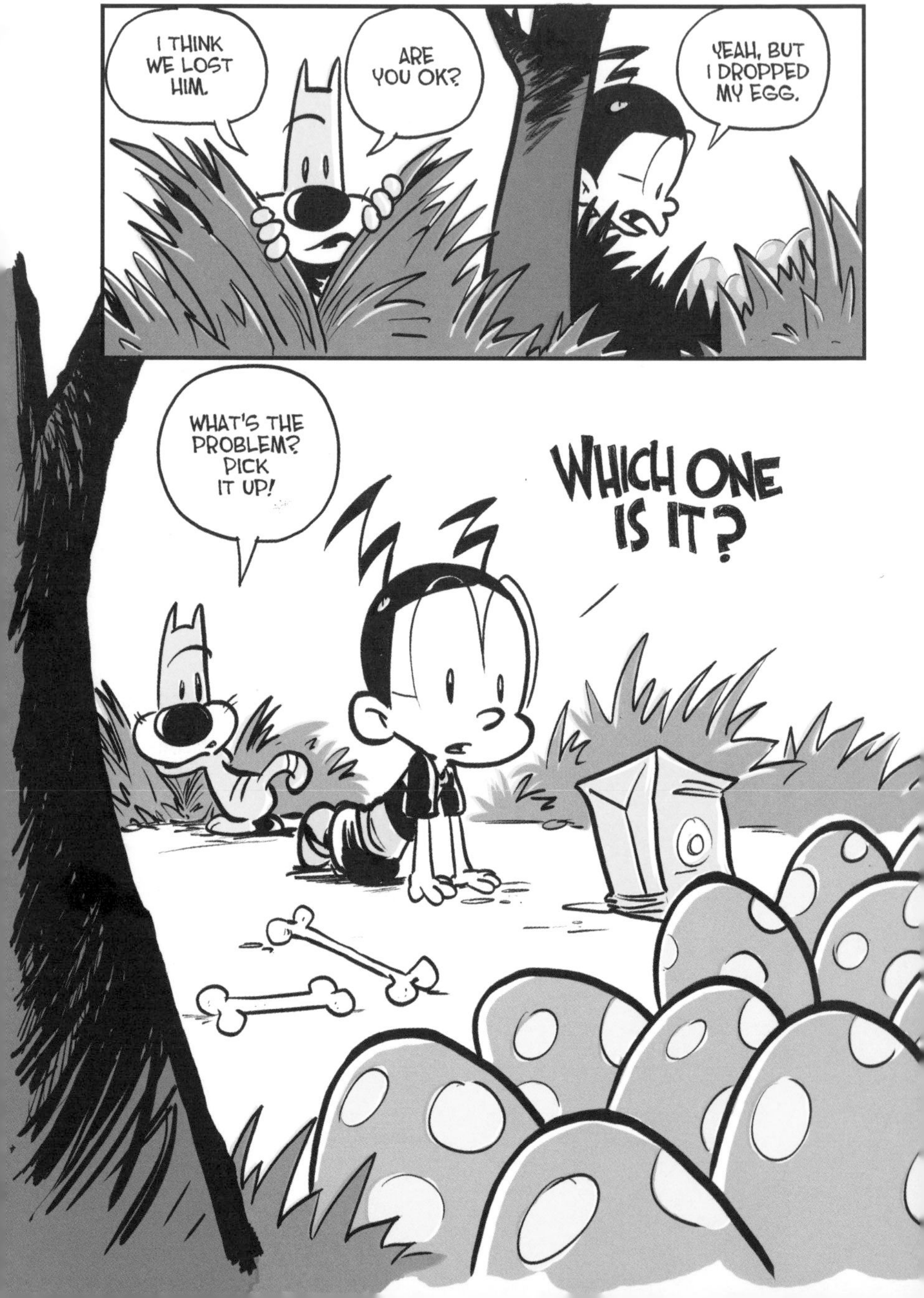
I THINK WE LOST HIM.
ARE YOU OK?
YEAH, BUT I DROPPED MY EGG.
WHAT'S THE PROBLEM? PICK IT UP!
WHICH ONE IS IT?

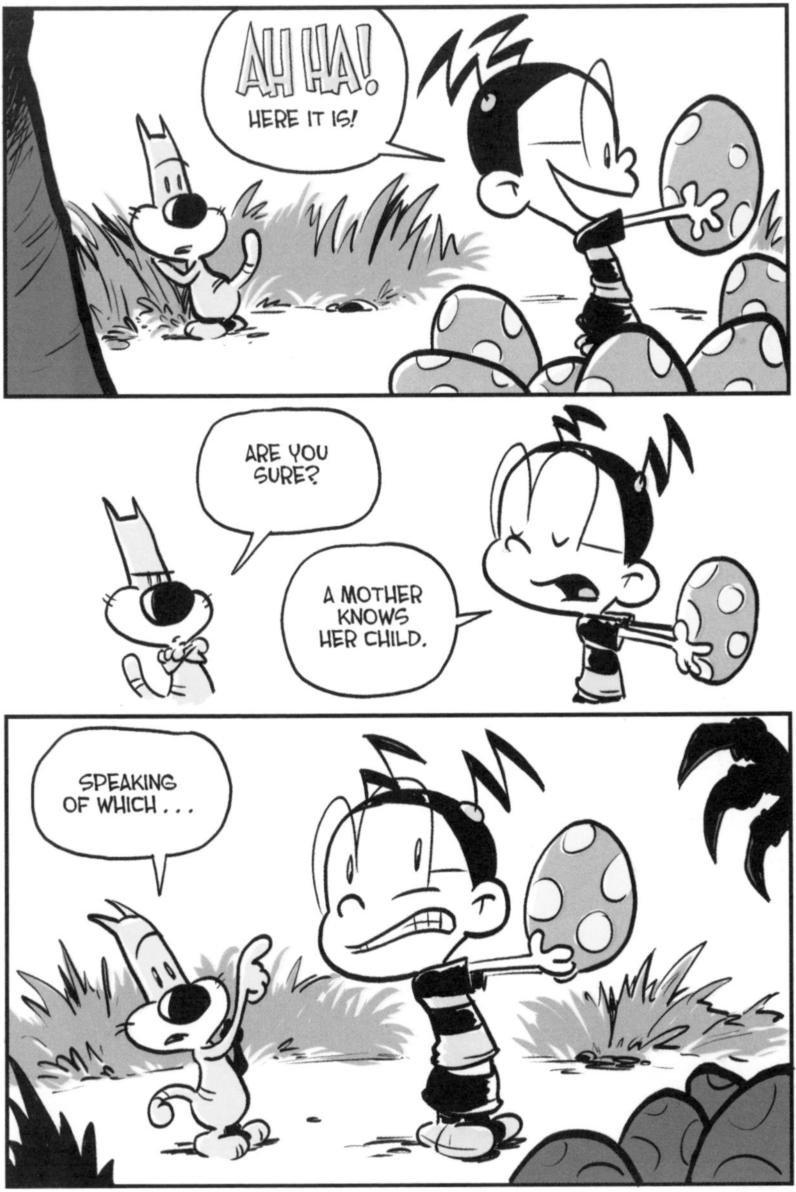
AH HA! HERE IT IS!
ARE YOU SURE?
A MOTHER KNOWS HER CHILD.
SPEAKING OF WHICH . . .

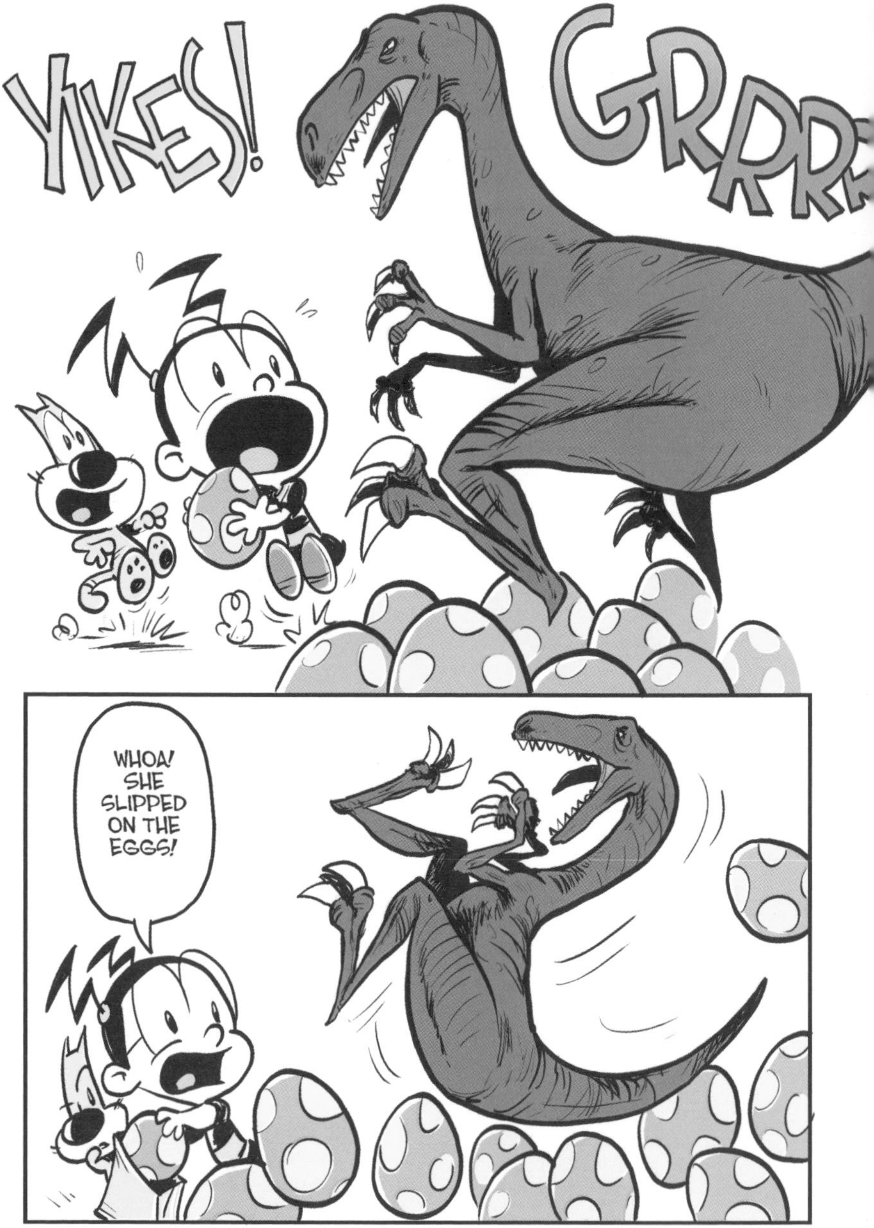
YIKES!
GRRR
WHOA! SHE SLIPPED ON THE EGGS!

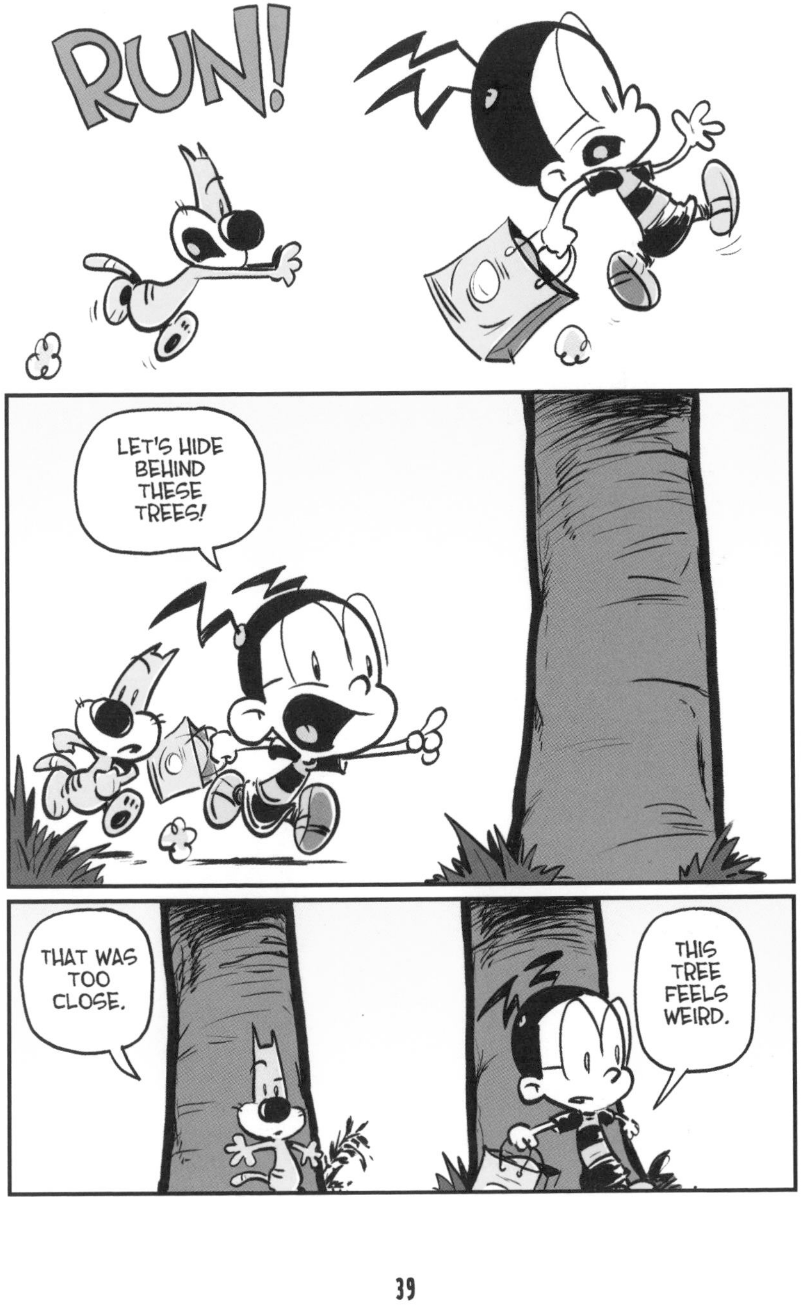
RUN!
LET'S HIDE BEHIND THESE TREES!
THAT WAS TOO CLOSE.
THIS TREE FEELS WEIRD.

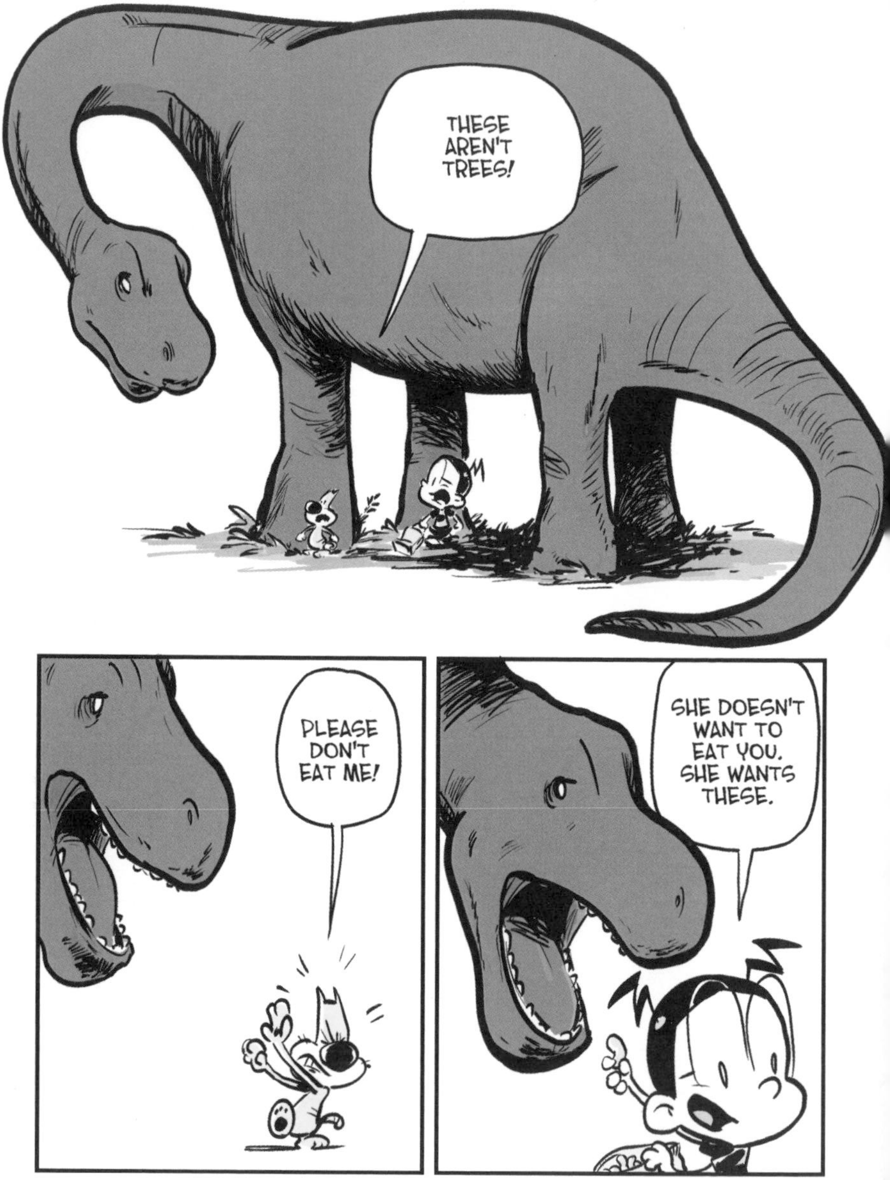
THESE AREN'T TREES!
PLEASE DON'T EAT ME!
SHE DOESN'T WANT TO EAT YOU. SHE WANTS THESE.

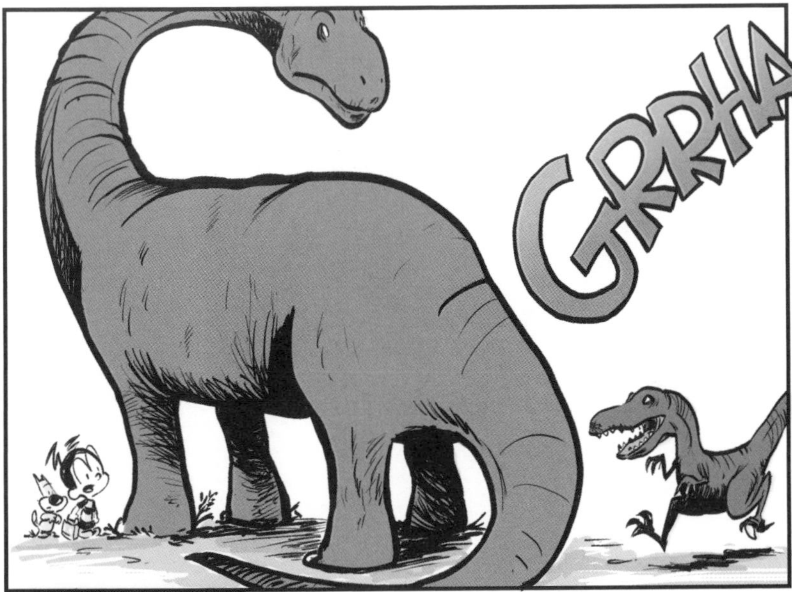
GRRHA

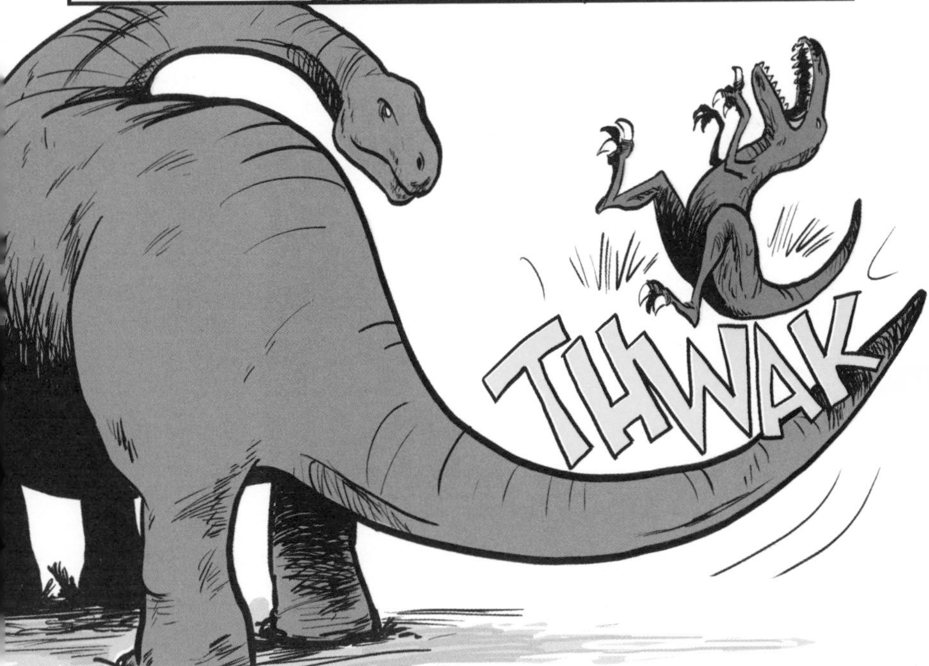
THWAK

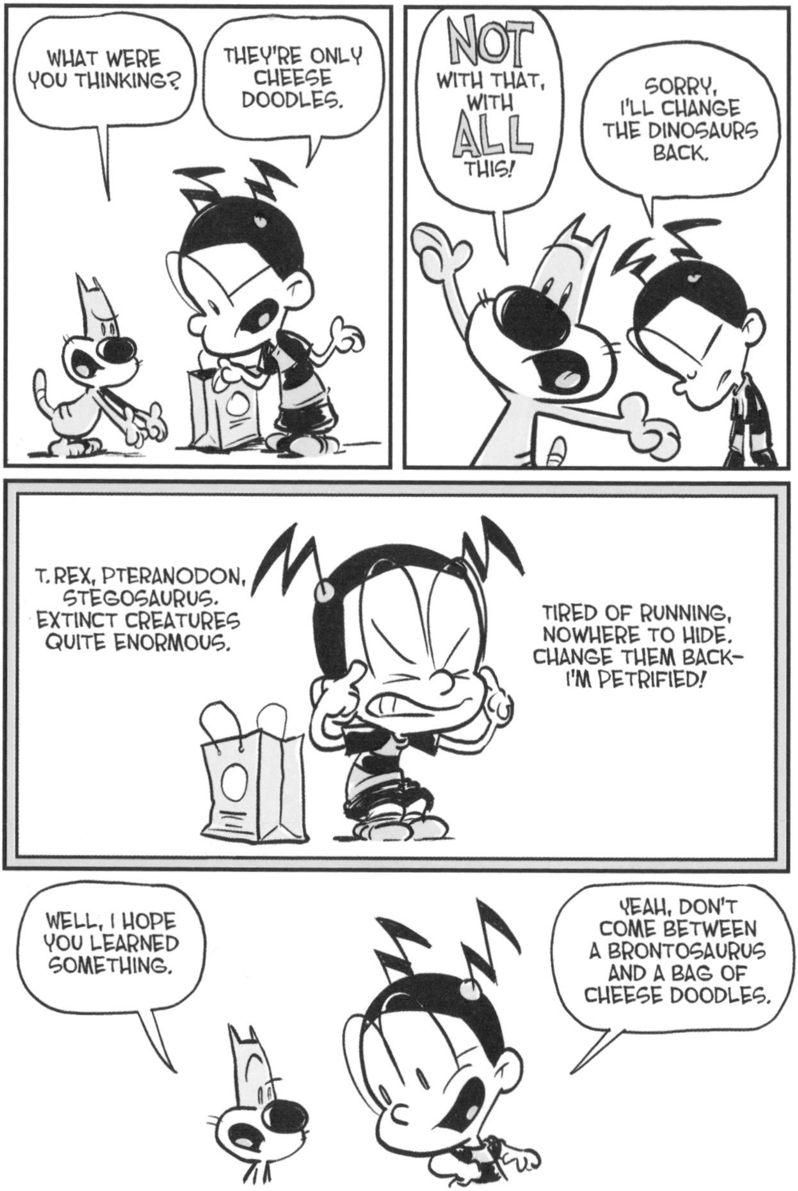
WHAT WERE YOU THINKING?
THEY'RE ONLY CHEESE DOODLES.
NOT WITH THAT, WITH ALL THIS!
SORRY, I'LL CHANGE THE DINOSAURS BACK.
T. REX, PTERANODON, STEGOSAURUS. EXTINCT CREATURES QUITE ENORMOUS.
TIRED OF RUNNING, NOWHERE TO HIDE. CHANGE THEM BACK- I'M PETRIFIED!
WELL, I HOPE YOU LEARNED SOMETHING.
YEAH, DON'T COME BETWEEN A BRONTOSAURUS AND A BAG OF CHEESE DOODLES.

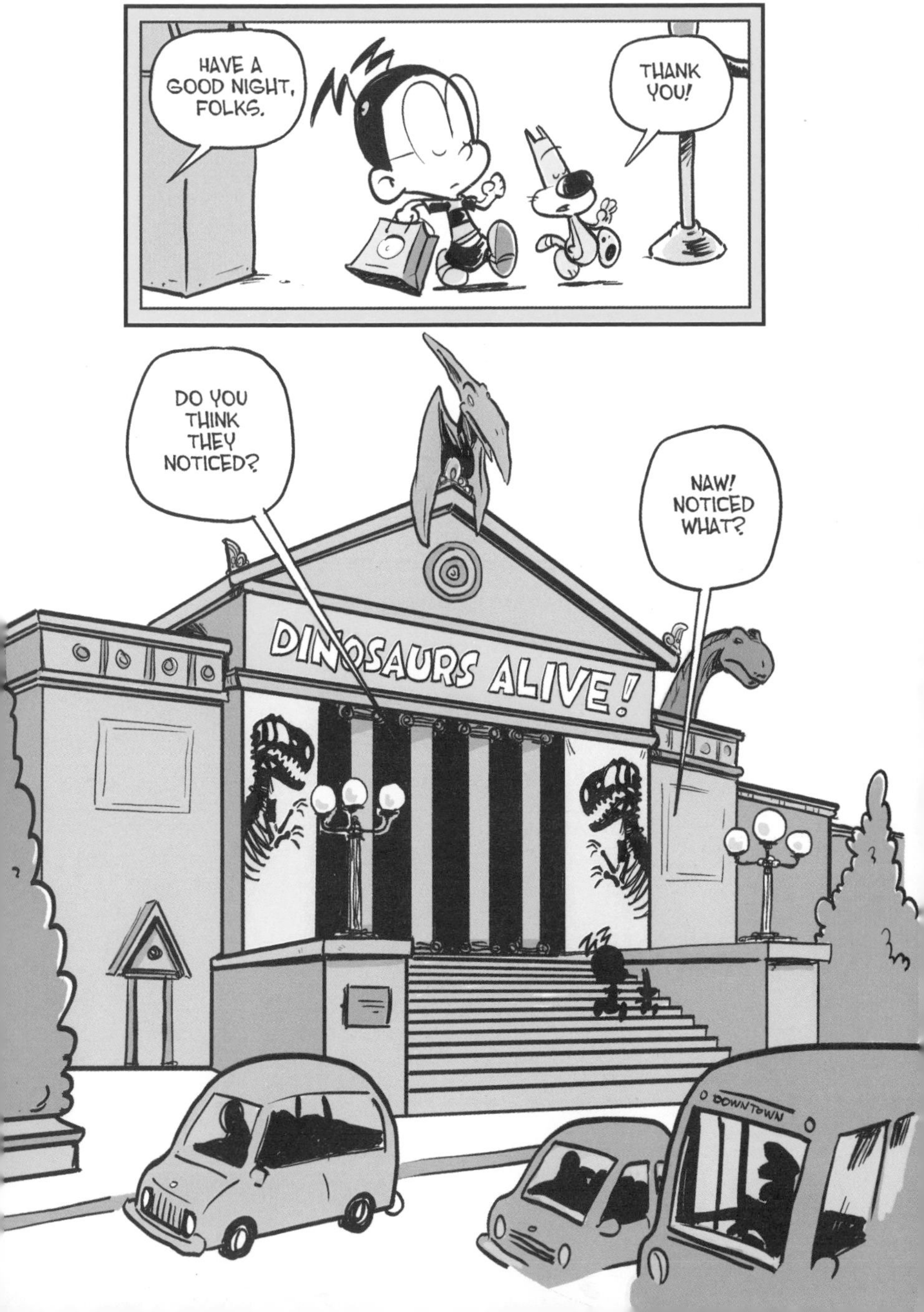
HAVE A GOOD NIGHT, FOLKS.
THANK YOU!
DO YOU THINK THEY NOTICED?
NAW! NOTICED WHAT?
DINOSAURS ALIVE!
DOWNTOWN

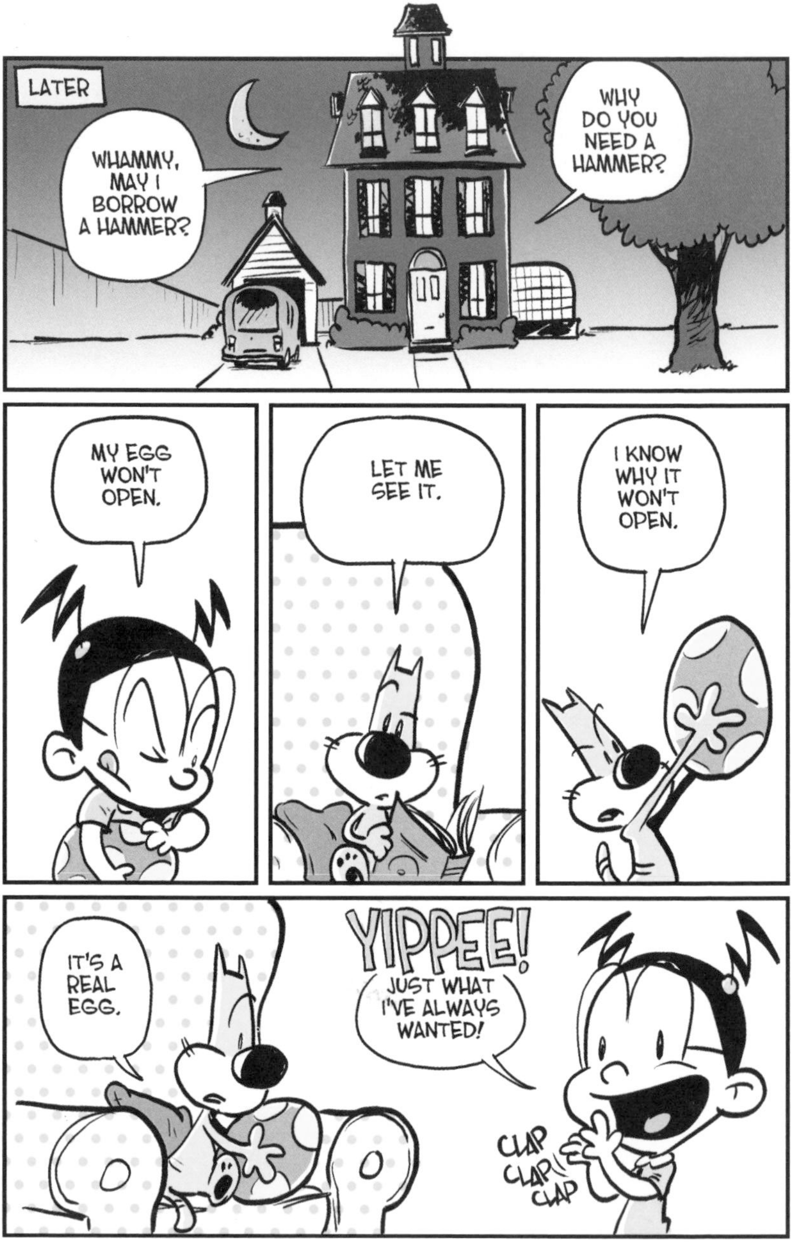
LATER
WHAMMY, MAY I BORROW A HAMMER?
WHY DO YOU NEED A HAMMER?
MY EGG WON'T OPEN.
LET ME SEE IT.
I KNOW WHY IT WON'T OPEN.
IT'S A REAL EGG.
YIPPEE!
JUST WHAT I'VE ALWAYS WANTED!
CLAP CLAP CLAP

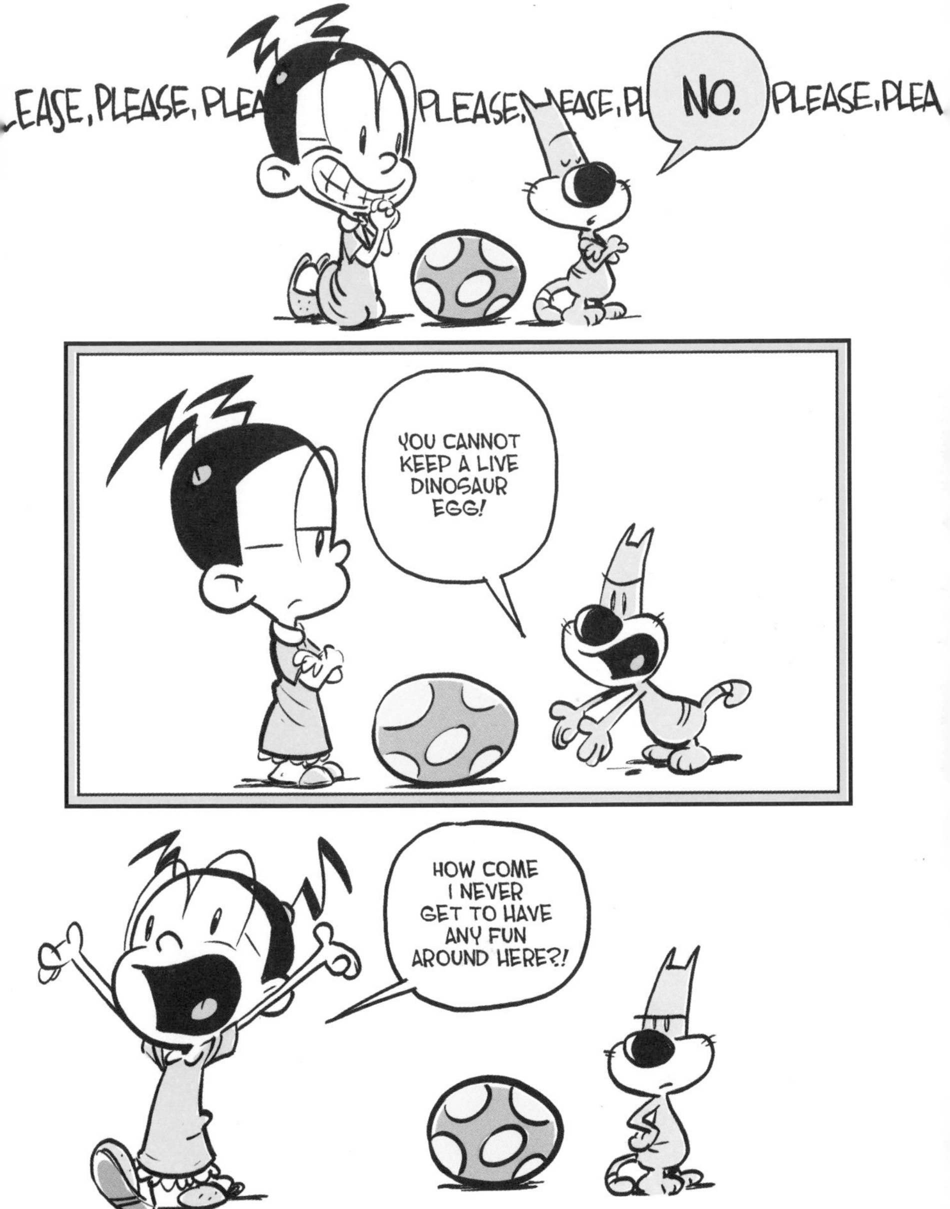
EASE, PLEASE, PLEA
PLEASE,
EASE, PL
NO.
PLEASE, PLEA
YOU CANNOT KEEP A LIVE DINOSAUR EGG!
HOW COME I NEVER GET TO HAVE ANY FUN AROUND HERE?!

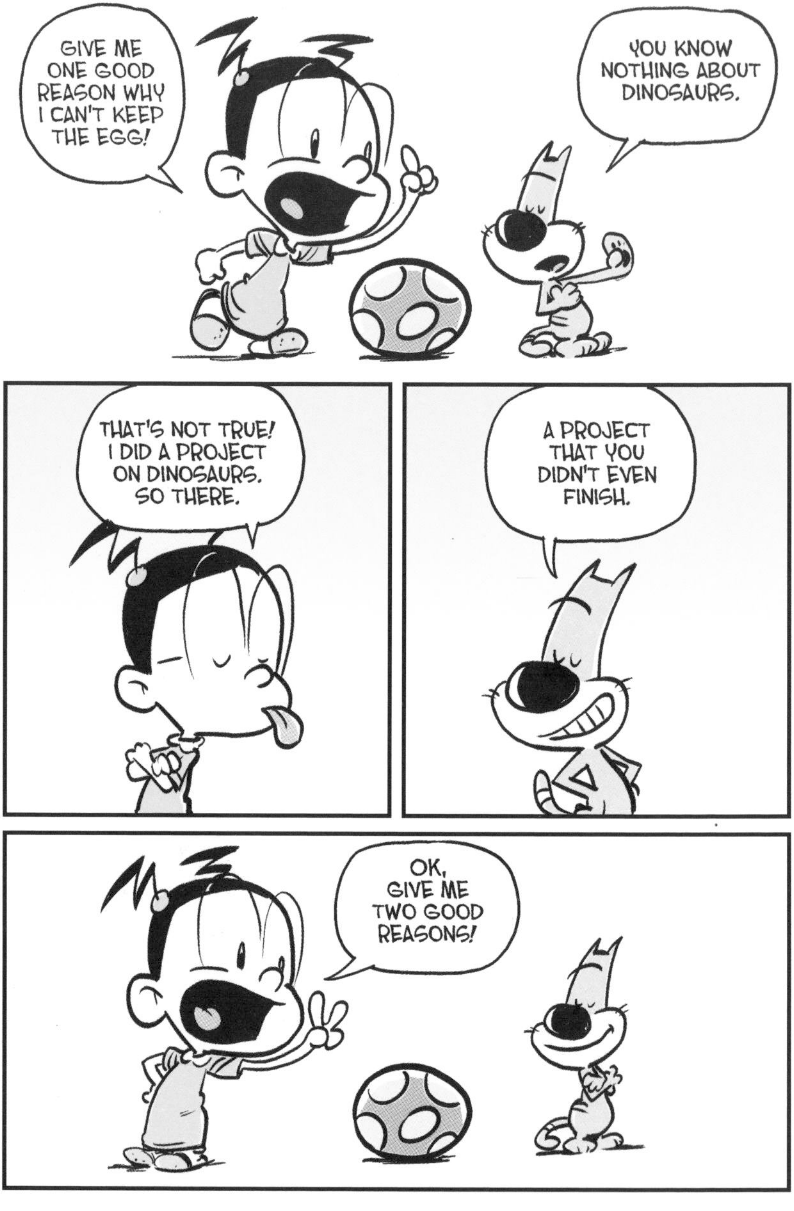
GIVE ME ONE GOOD REASON WHY I CAN'T KEEP THE EGG!
YOU KNOW NOTHING ABOUT DINOSAURS.
THAT'S NOT TRUE! I DID A PROJECT ON DINOSAURS. SO THERE.
A PROJECT THAT YOU DIDN'T EVEN FINISH.
OK, GIVE ME TWO GOOD REASONS!

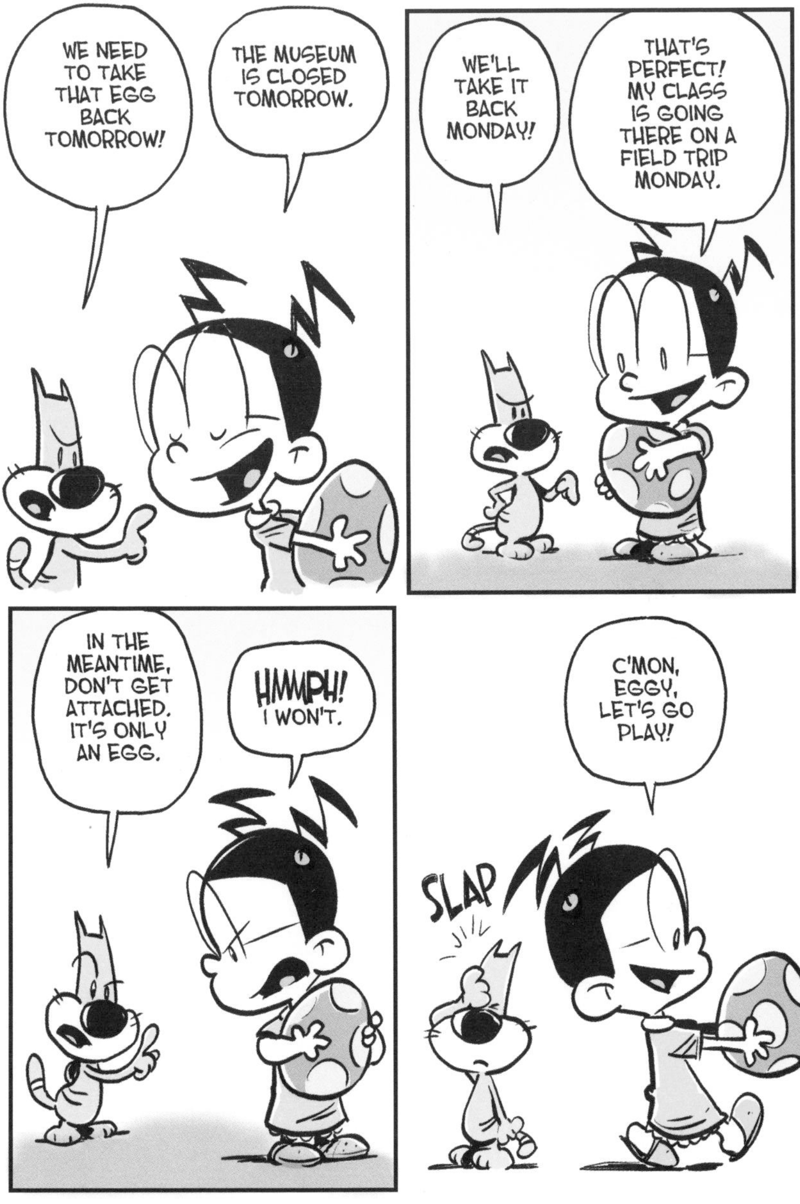
WE NEED TO TAKE THAT EGG BACK TOMORROW!
THE MUSEUM IS CLOSED TOMORROW.
WE'LL TAKE IT BACK MONDAY!
THAT'S PERFECT! MY CLASS IS GOING THERE ON A FIELD TRIP MONDAY.
IN THE MEANTIME, DON'T GET ATTACHED. IT'S ONLY AN EGG.
HMMPH! I WON'T.
C'MON, EGGY, LET'S GO PLAY!
SLAP

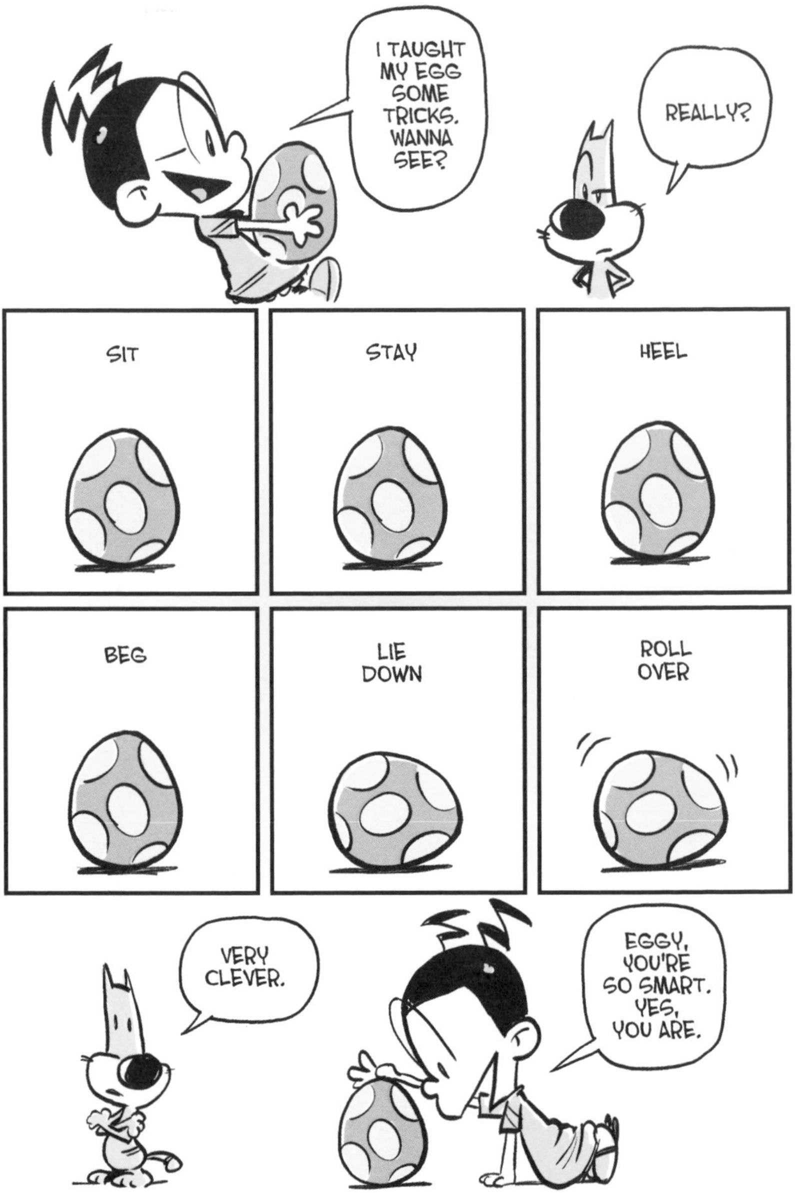

I TAUGHT MY EGG SOME TRICKS. WANNA SEE?
REALLY?
SIT
STAY
HEEL
BEG
LIE DOWN
ROLL OVER
VERY CLEVER.
EGGY, YOU'RE SO SMART. YES, YOU ARE.

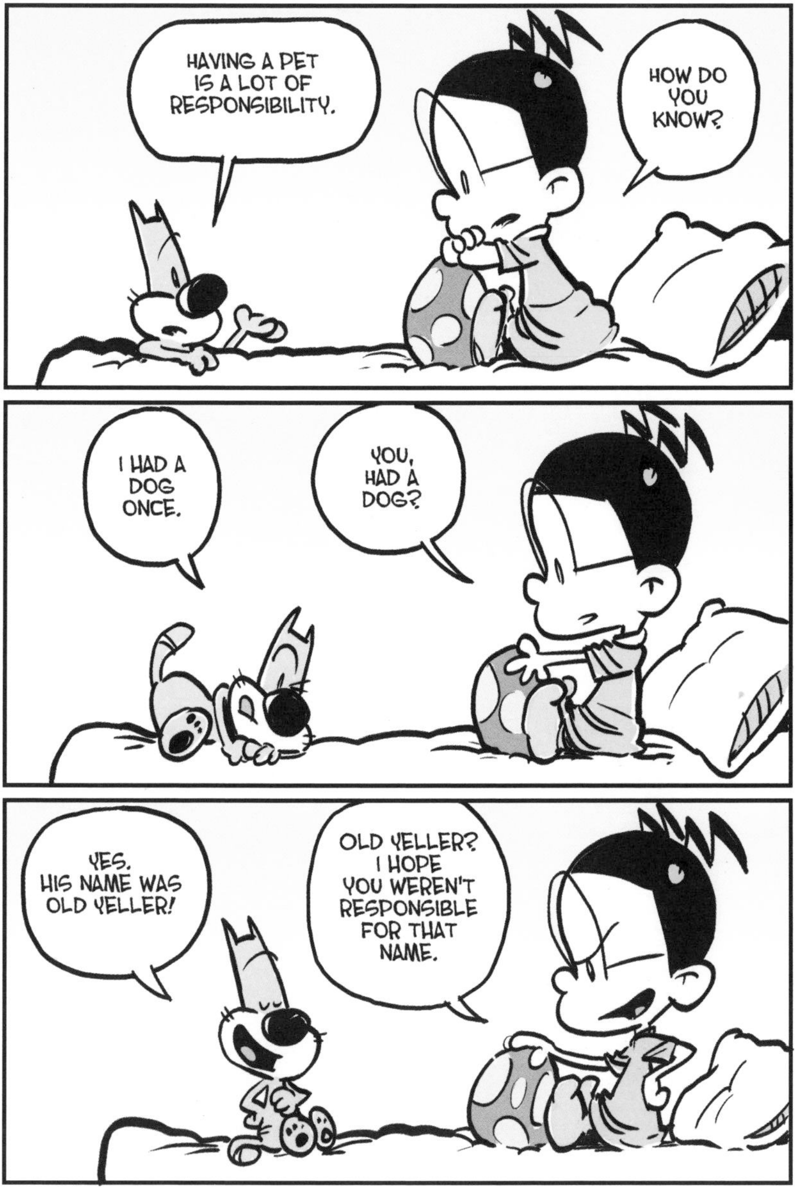
HAVING A PET IS A LOT OF RESPONSIBILITY.
HOW DO YOU KNOW?
I HAD A DOG ONCE.
YOU, HAD A DOG?
YES. HIS NAME WAS OLD YELLER!
OLD YELLER? I HOPE YOU WEREN'T RESPONSIBLE FOR THAT NAME.

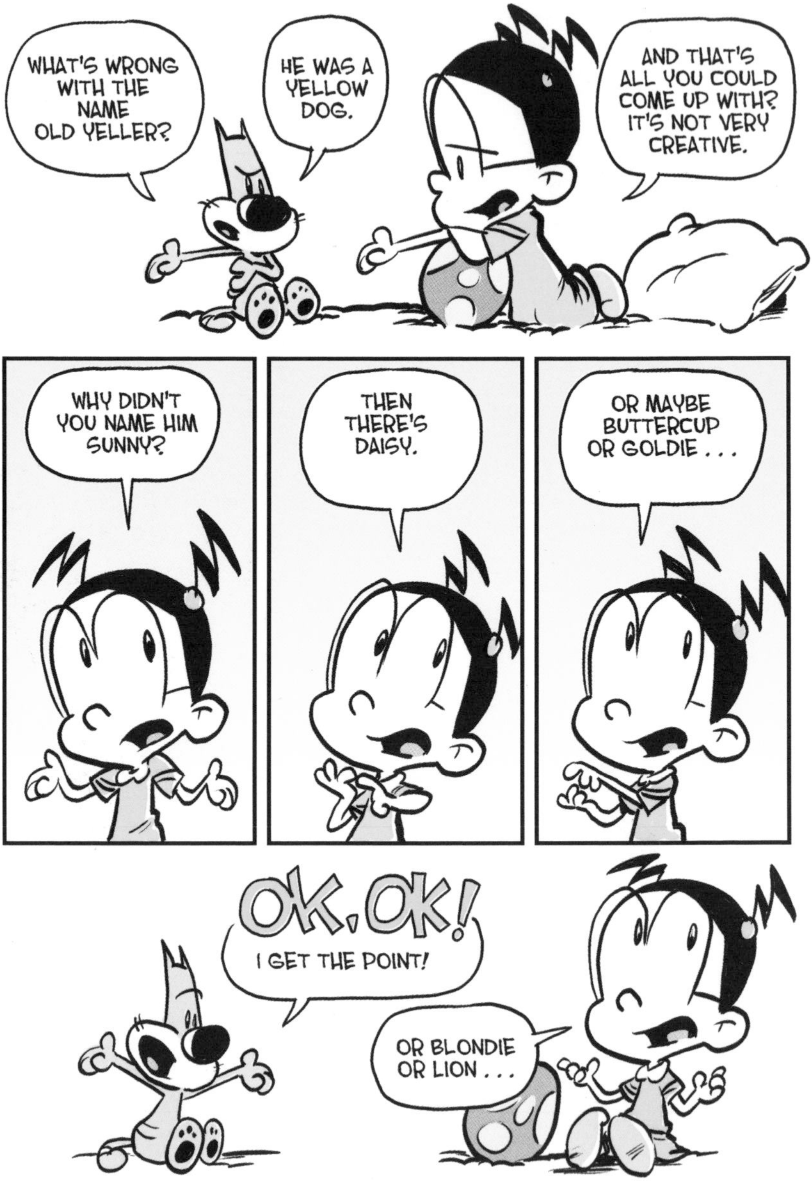
WHAT'S WRONG WITH THE NAME OLD YELLER?
HE WAS A YELLOW DOG.
AND THAT'S ALL YOU COULD COME UP WITH? IT'S NOT VERY CREATIVE.
WHY DIDN'T YOU NAME HIM SUNNY?
THEN THERE'S DAISY.
OR MAYBE BUTTERCUP OR GOLDIE . . .
OK, OK! I GET THE POINT!
OR BLONDIE OR LION . . .

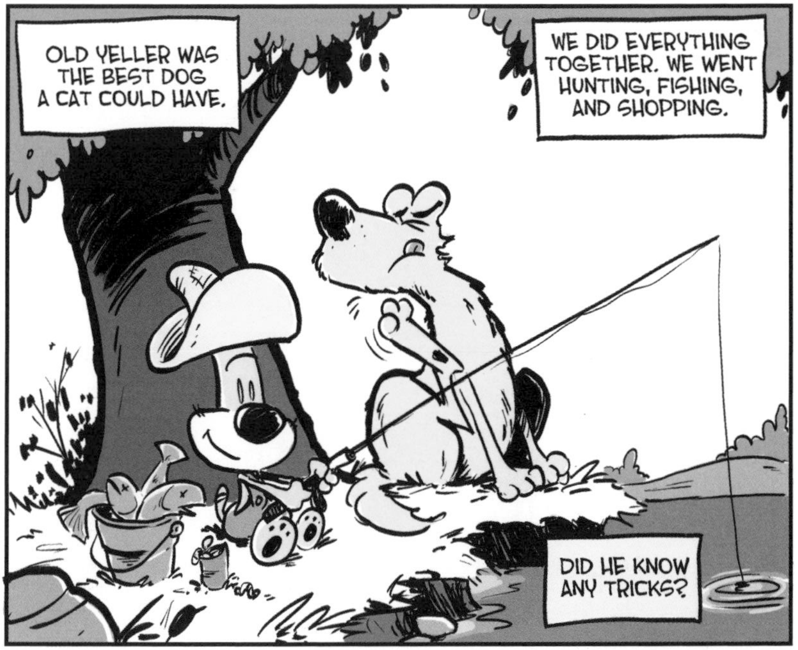
OLD YELLER WAS THE BEST DOG A CAT COULD HAVE.
WE DID EVERYTHING TOGETHER. WE WENT HUNTING, FISHING, AND SHOPPING.
DID HE KNOW ANY TRICKS?

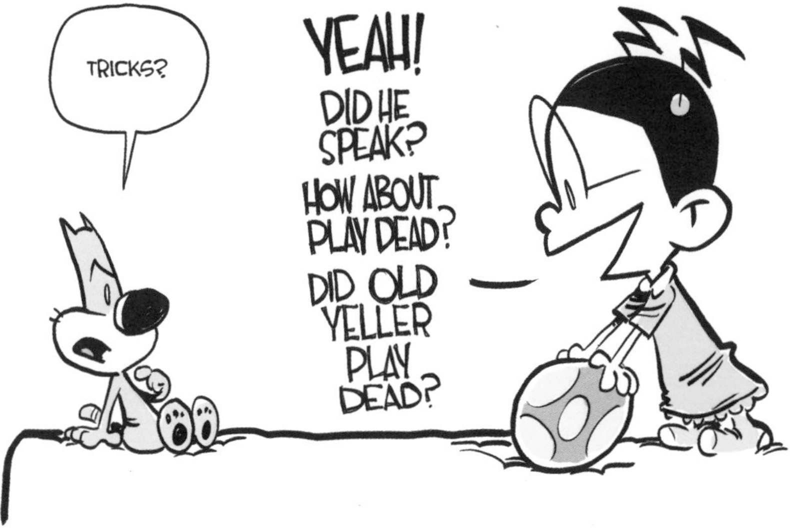
TRICKS?
YEAH!
DID HE SPEAK?
HOW ABOUT PLAY DEAD?
DID OLD YELLER PLAY DEAD?

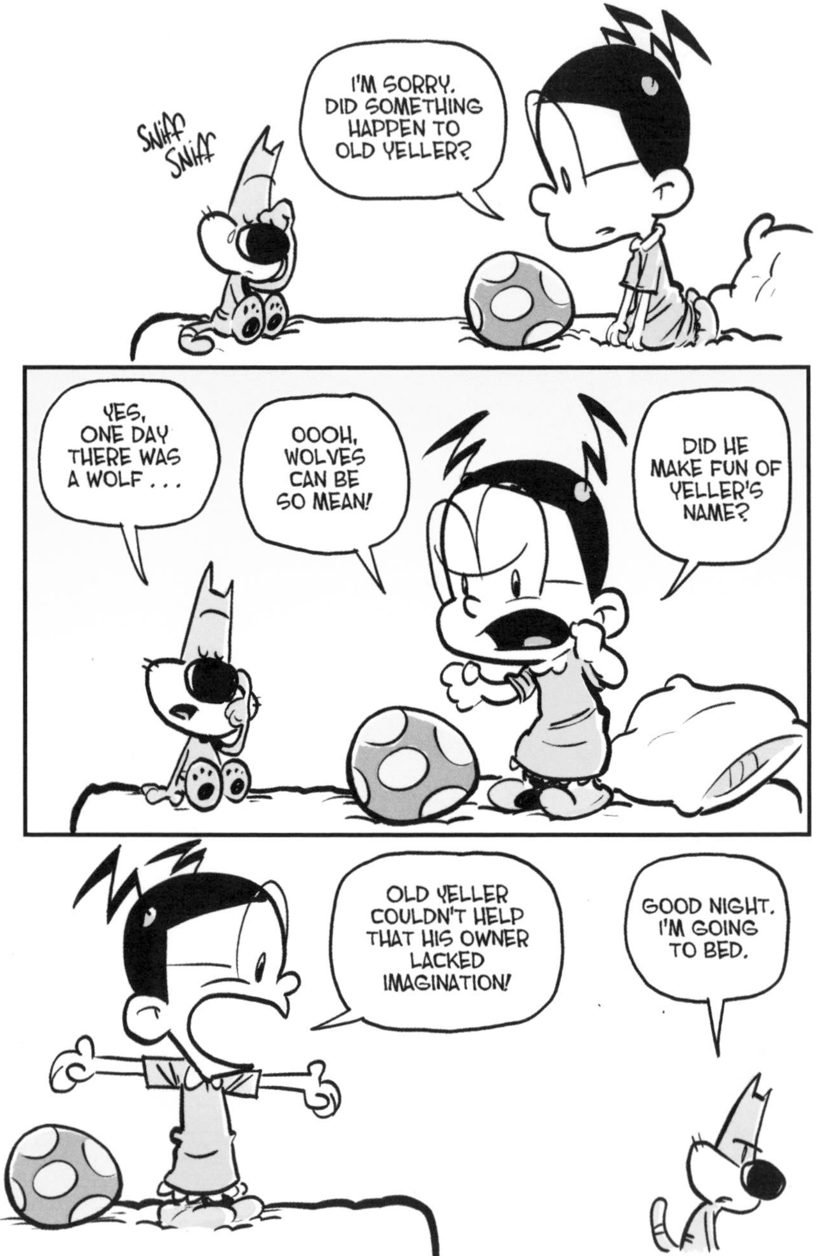

SNIFF SNIFF
I'M SORRY. DID SOMETHING HAPPEN TO OLD YELLER?
YES, ONE DAY THERE WAS A WOLF . . .
OOOH, WOLVES CAN BE SO MEAN!
DID HE MAKE FUN OF YELLER'S NAME?
OLD YELLER COULDN'T HELP THAT HIS OWNER LACKED IMAGINATION!
GOOD NIGHT. I'M GOING TO BED.

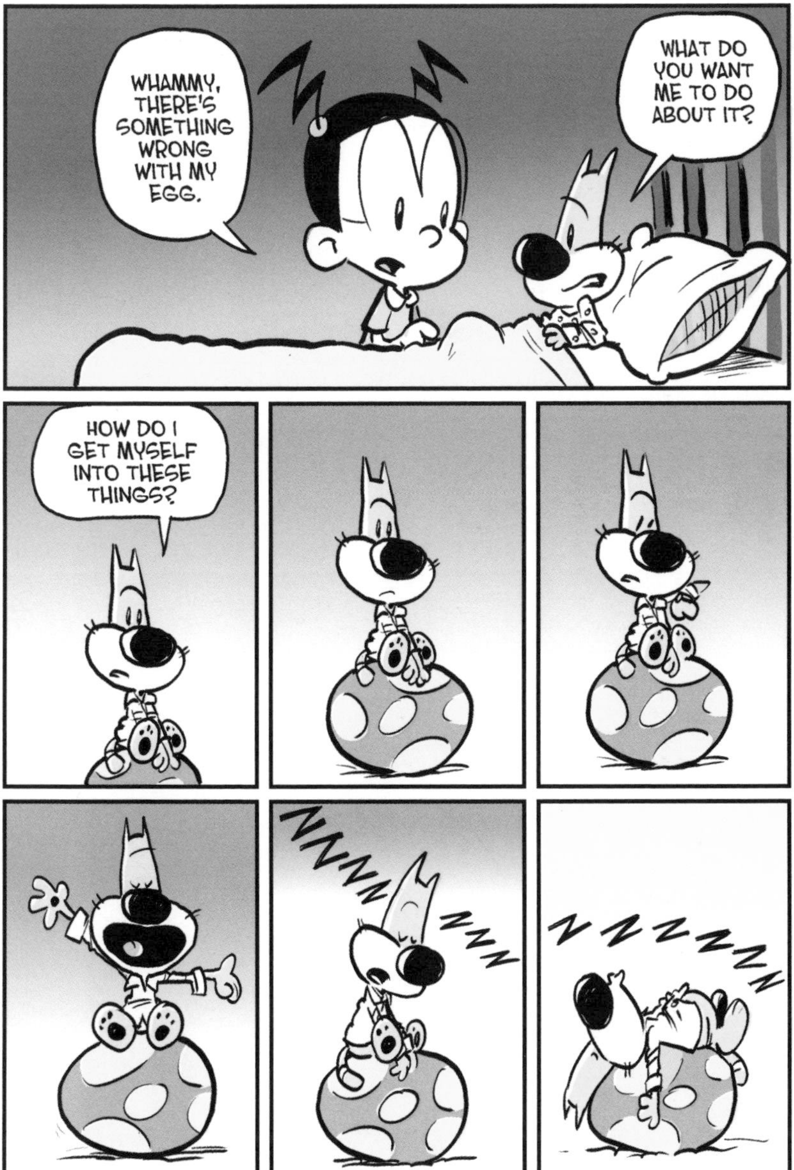
WHAMMY, THERE'S SOMETHING WRONG WITH MY EGG.
WHAT DO YOU WANT ME TO DO ABOUT IT?
HOW DO I GET MYSELF INTO THESE THINGS?
NNNNN
ZZZZZ
ZZZZZZZ

The NEXT MORNING

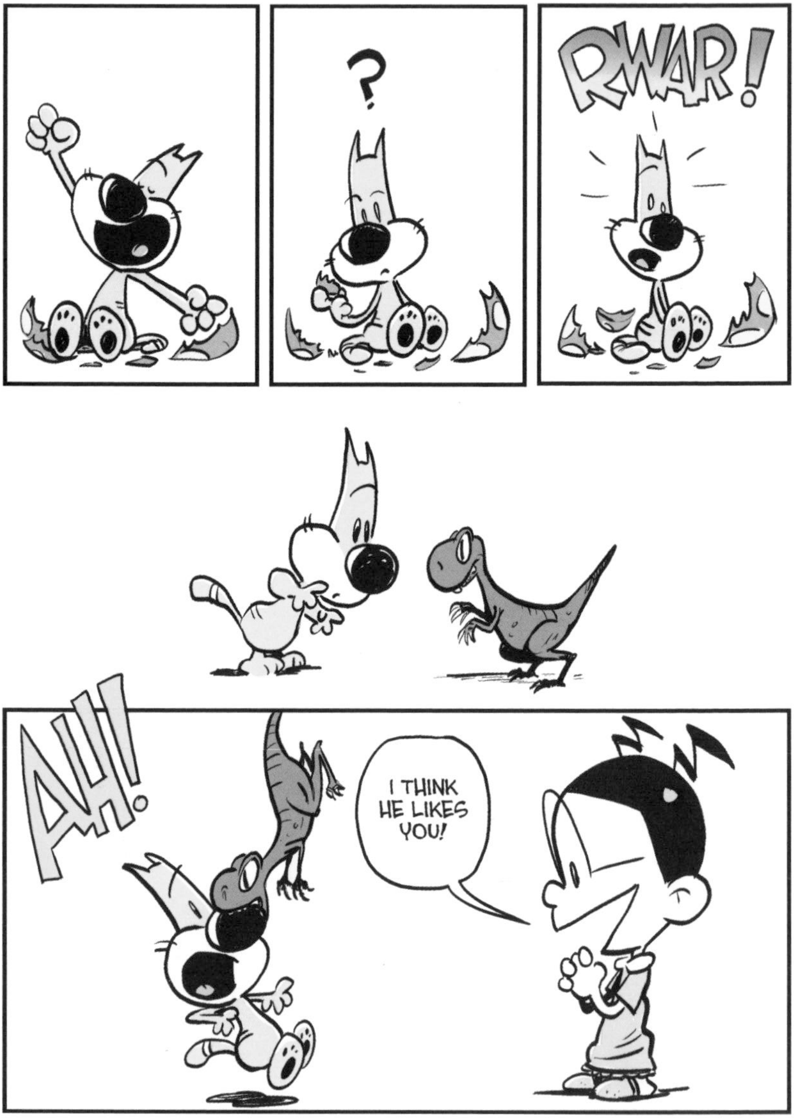
?
RWAR!
AH!
I THINK HE LIKES YOU!

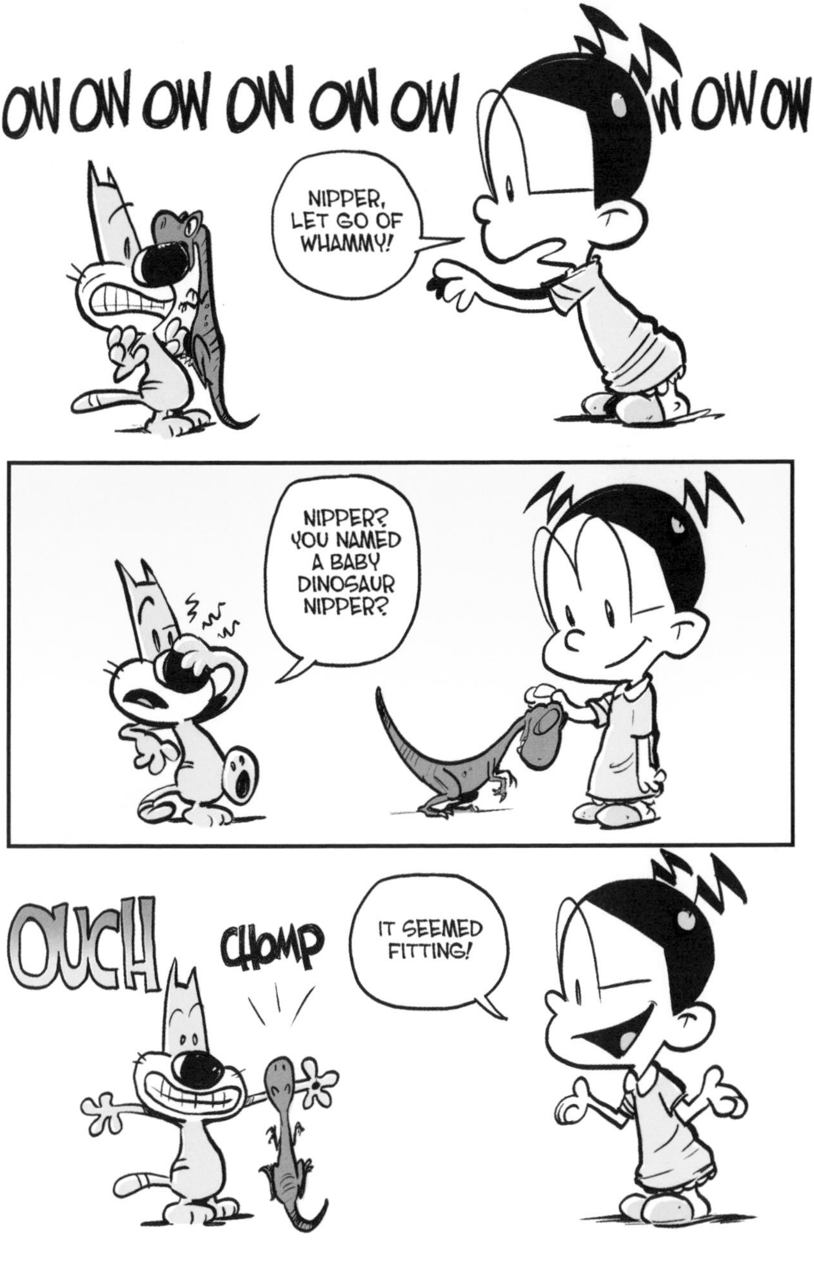
OW OW OW OW OW OW OW OW OW
NIPPER, LET GO OF WHAMMY!
NIPPER? YOU NAMED A BABY DINOSAUR NIPPER?
OUCH
CHOMP
IT SEEMED FITTING!

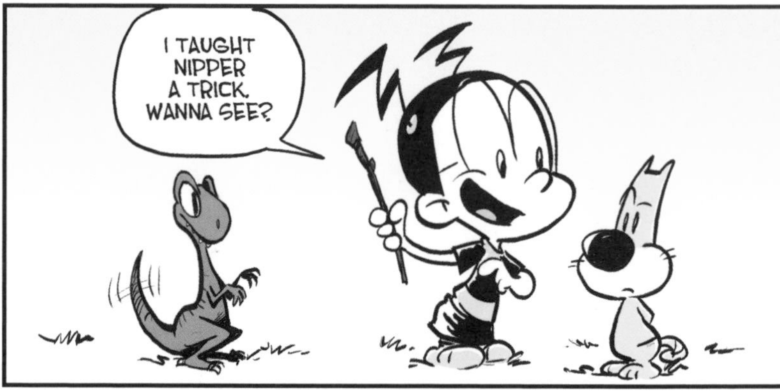
I TAUGHT NIPPER A TRICK. WANNA SEE?

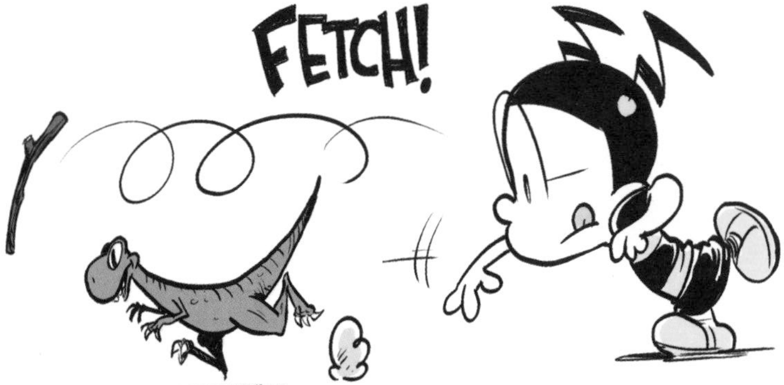
FETCH!

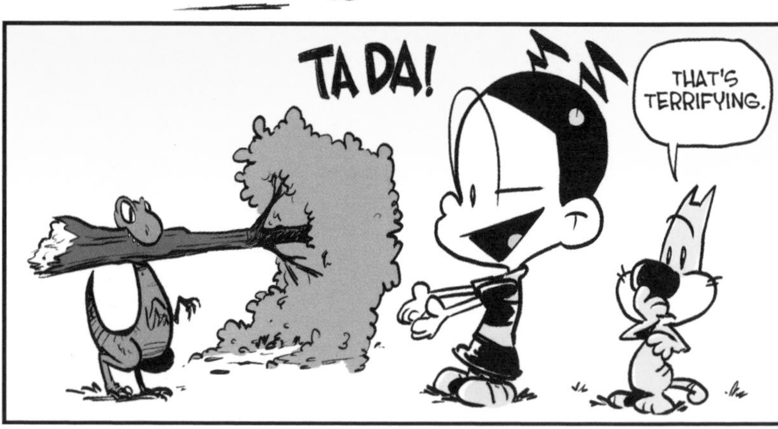
TA DA!
THAT'S TERRIFYING.

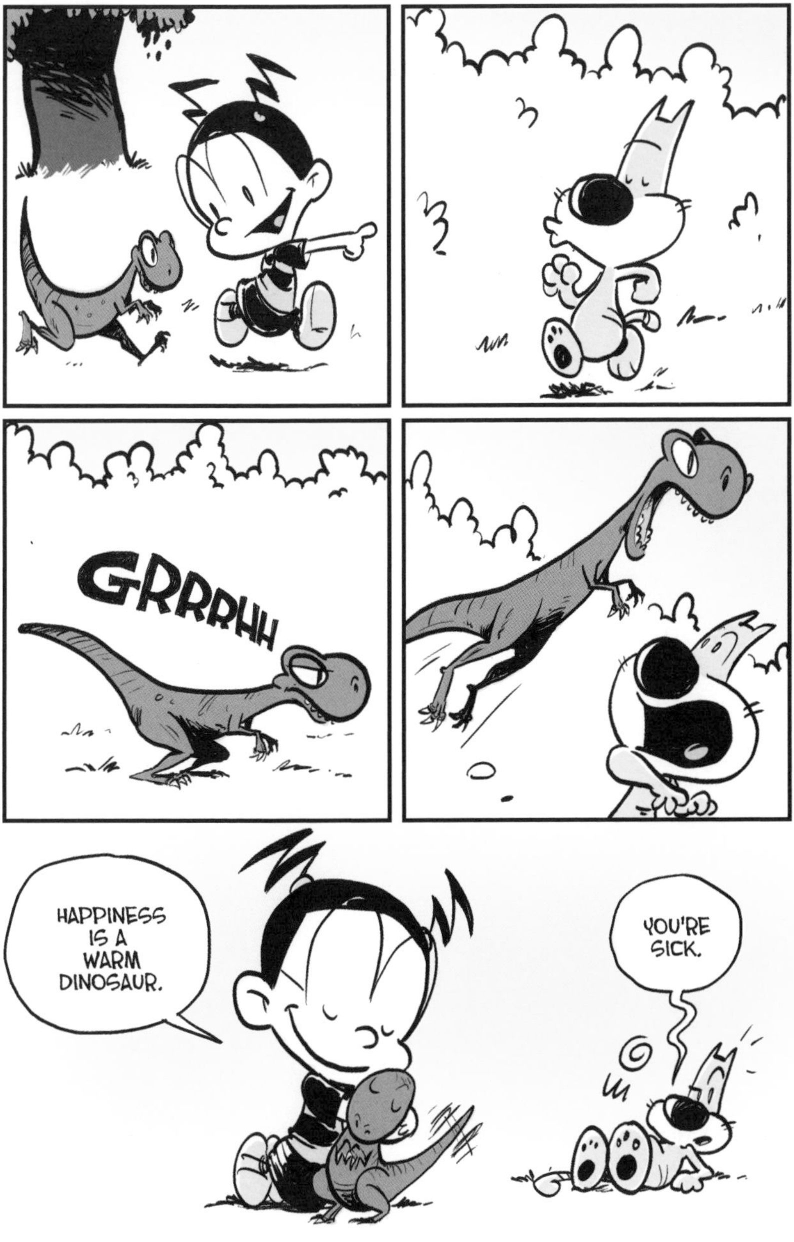
GRRRHH
HAPPINESS IS A WARM DINOSAUR.
YOU'RE SICK.

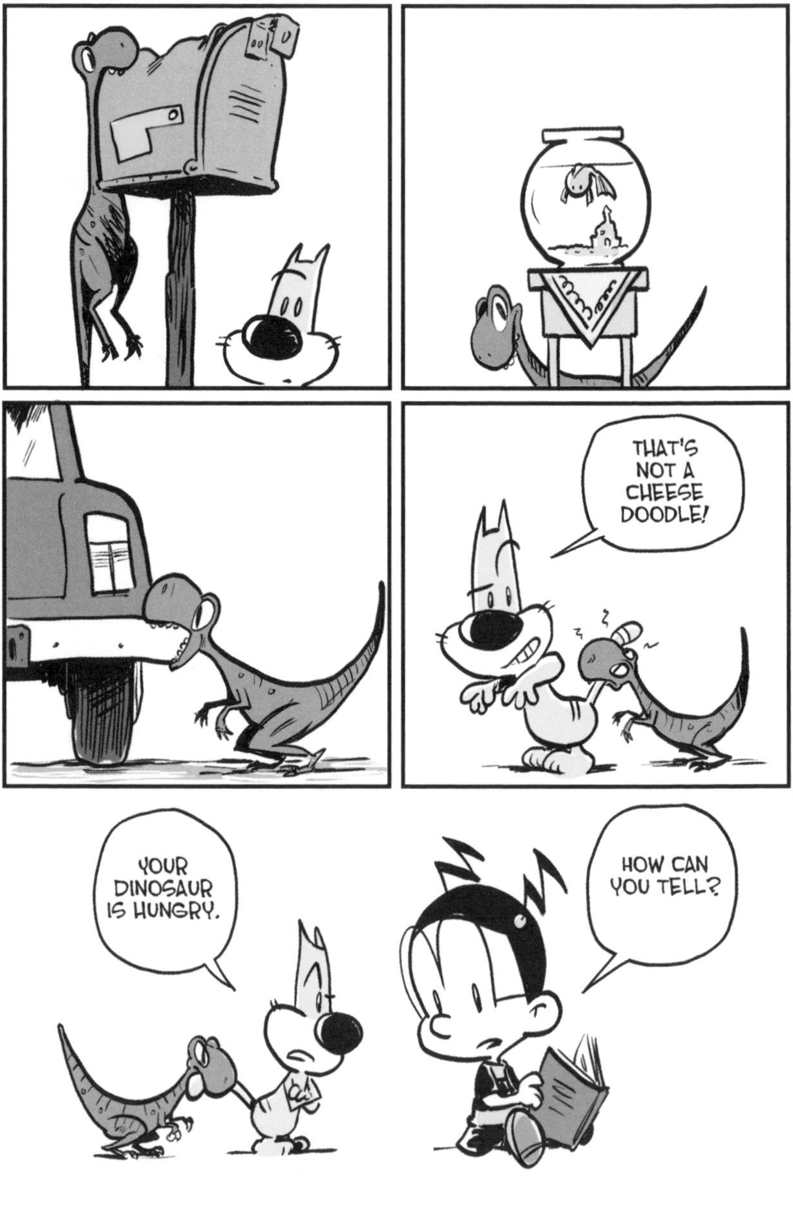
THAT'S NOT A CHEESE DOODLE!
YOUR DINOSAUR IS HUNGRY.
HOW CAN YOU TELL?

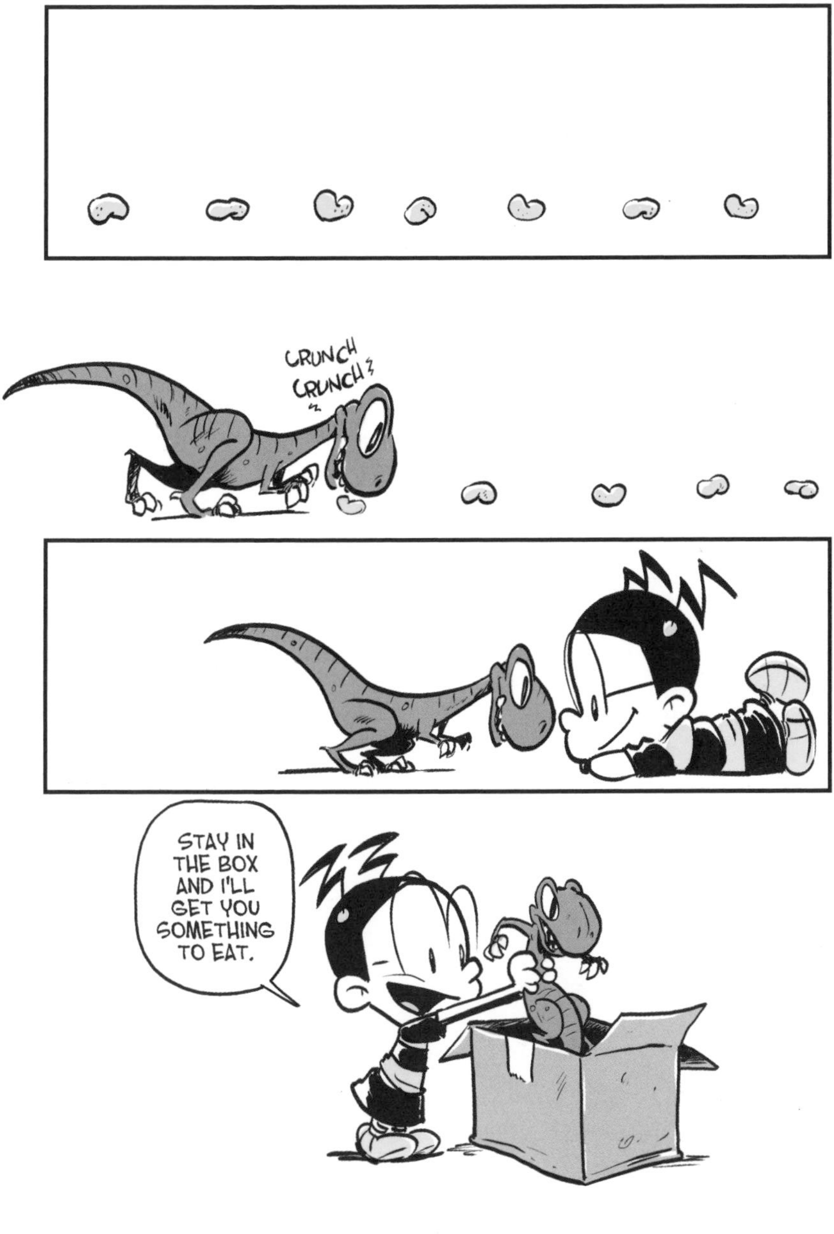
CRUNCH
CRUNCH
STAY IN THE BOX AND I'LL GET YOU SOMETHING TO EAT.

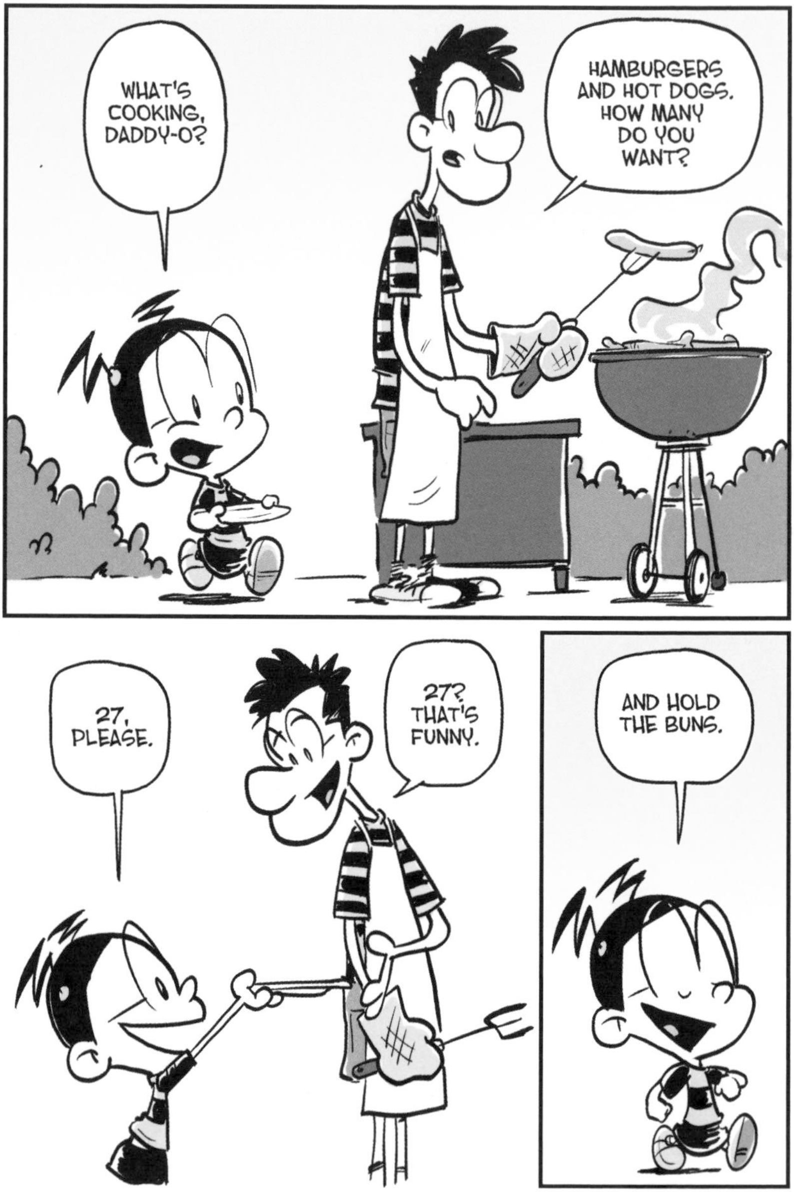
WHAT'S COOKING, DADDY-O?
HAMBURGERS AND HOT DOGS. HOW MANY DO YOU WANT?
27, PLEASE.
27? THAT'S FUNNY.
AND HOLD THE BUNS.

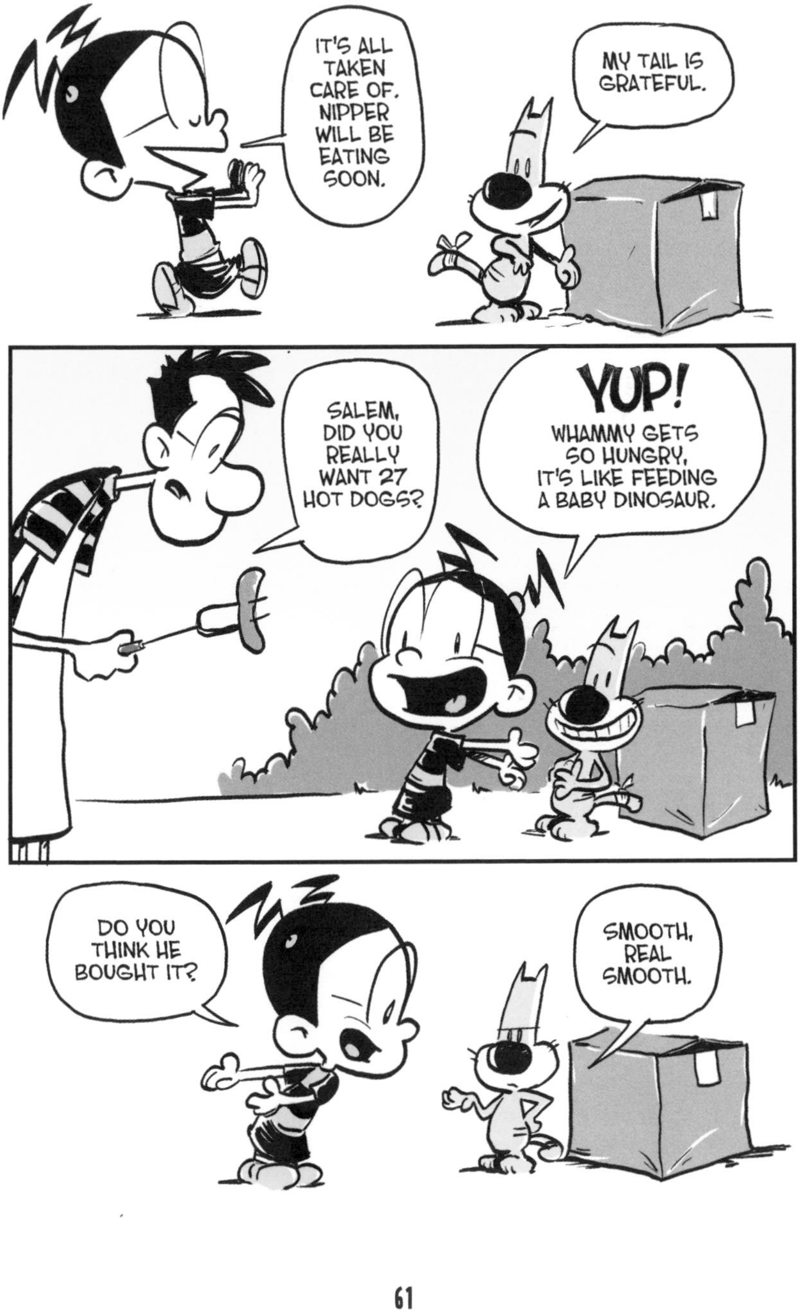
IT'S ALL TAKEN CARE OF. NIPPER WILL BE EATING SOON.
MY TAIL IS GRATEFUL.
SALEM, DID YOU REALLY WANT 27 HOT DOGS?
YUP! WHAMMY GETS SO HUNGRY, IT'S LIKE FEEDING A BABY DINOSAUR.
DO YOU THINK HE BOUGHT IT?
SMOOTH, REAL SMOOTH.

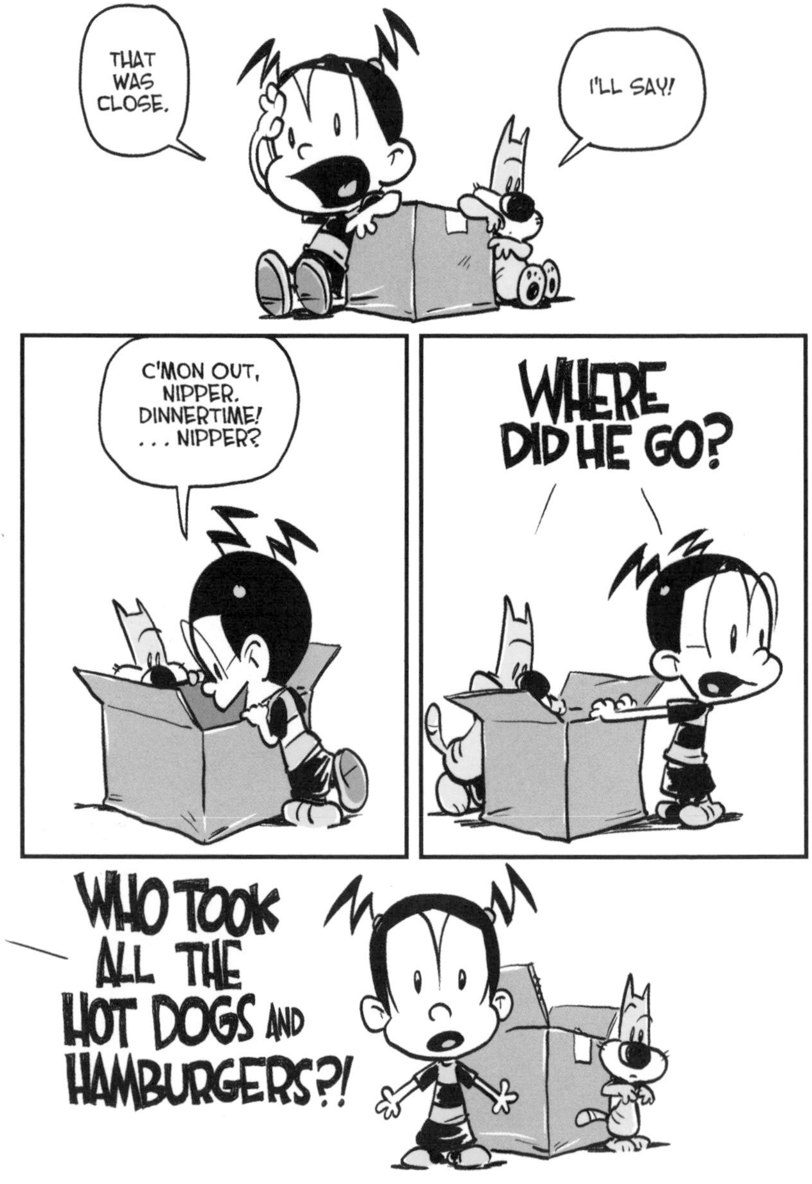
THAT WAS CLOSE.
I'LL SAY!
C'MON OUT, NIPPER. DINNERTIME! . . . NIPPER?
WHERE DID HE GO?
WHO TOOK ALL THE HOT DOGS AND HAMBURGERS?!

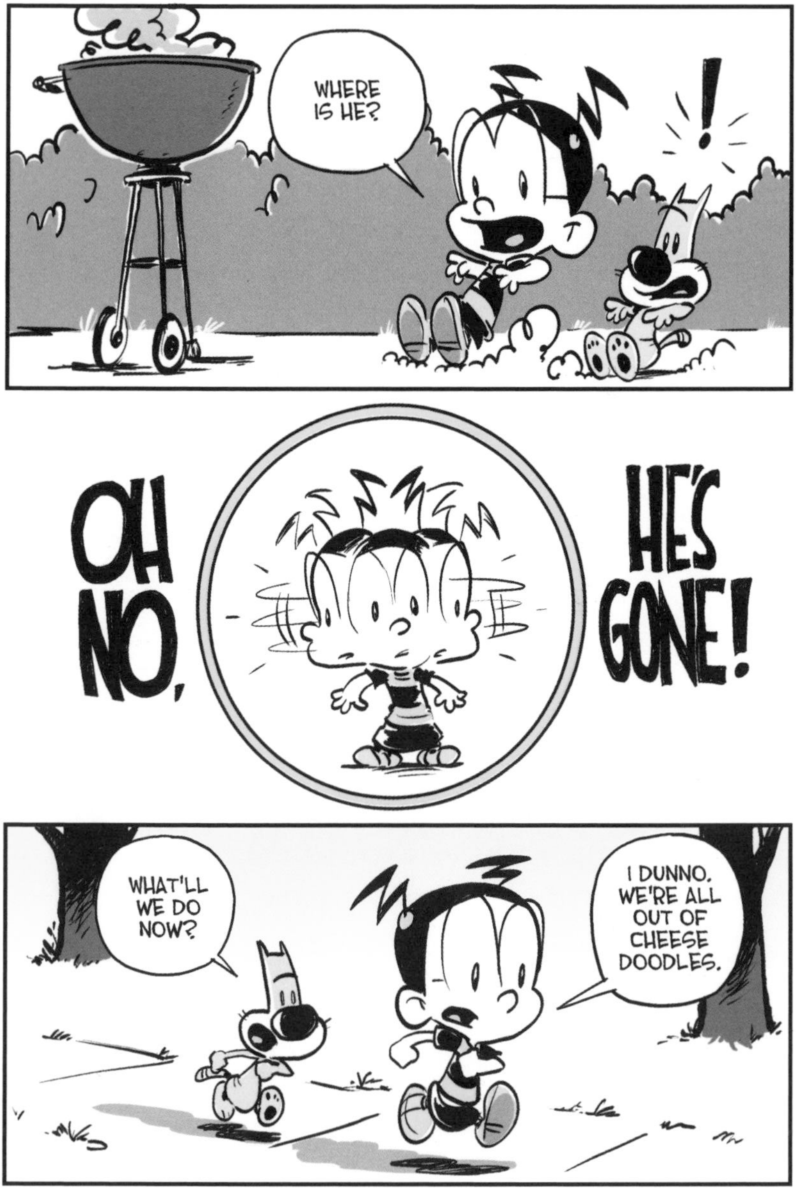
WHERE IS HE?
!
OH NO,
HE'S GONE!
WHAT'LL WE DO NOW?
I DUNNO. WE'RE ALL OUT OF CHEESE DOODLES.

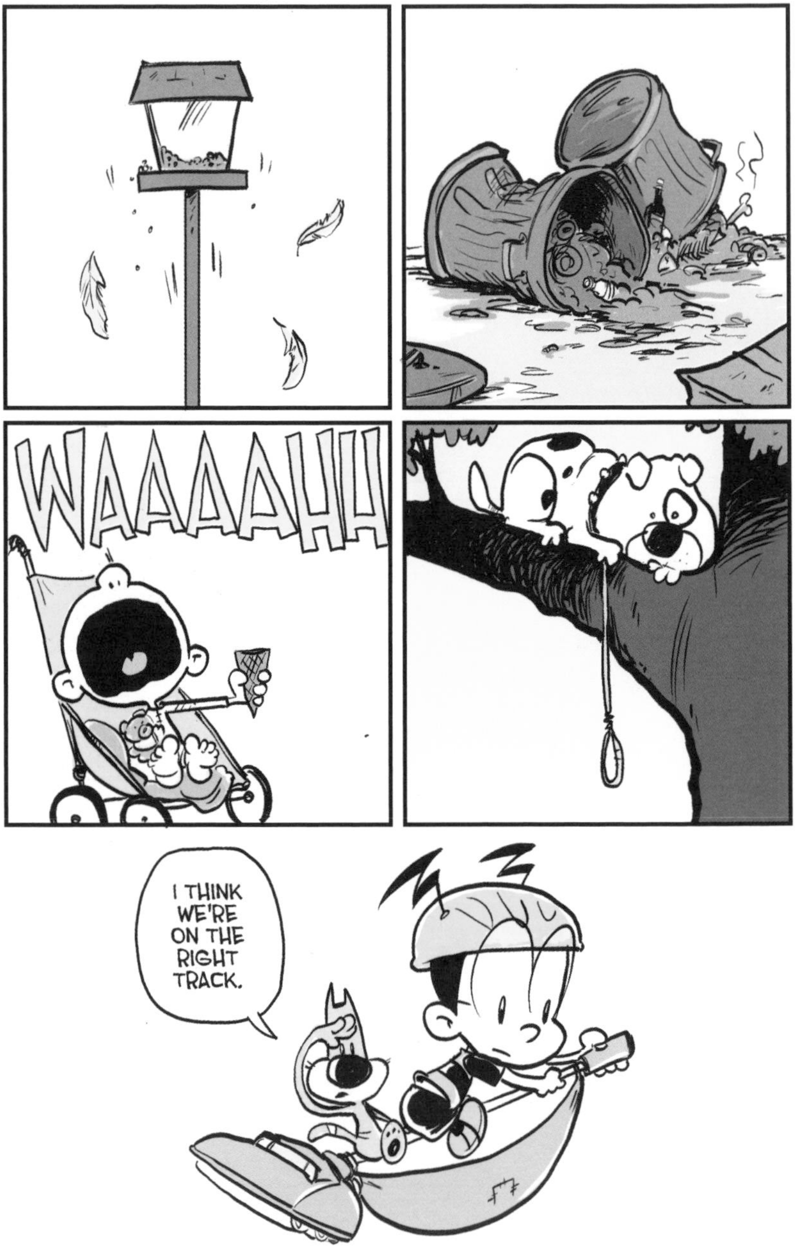
WAAAAHH
I THINK WE'RE ON THE RIGHT TRACK.

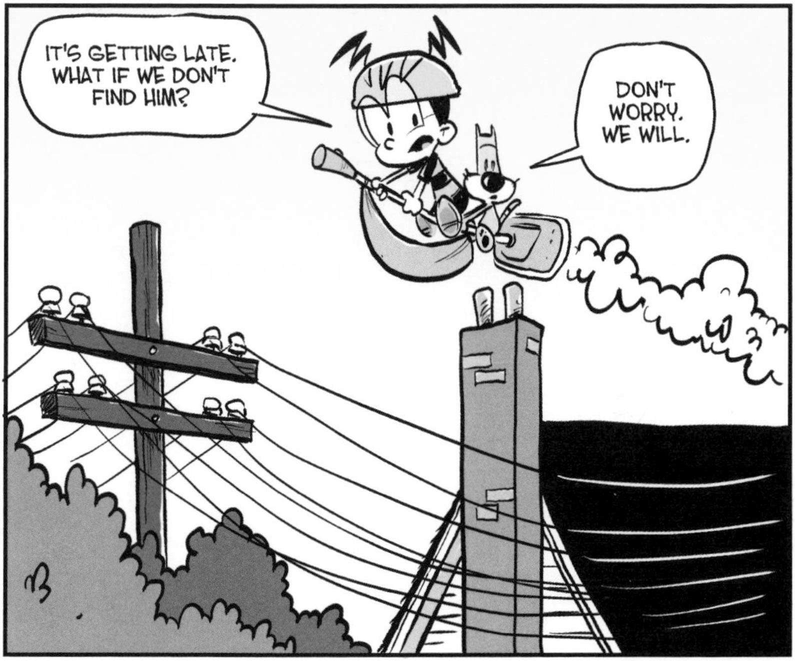
IT'S GETTING LATE. WHAT IF WE DON'T FIND HIM?
DON'T WORRY. WE WILL.

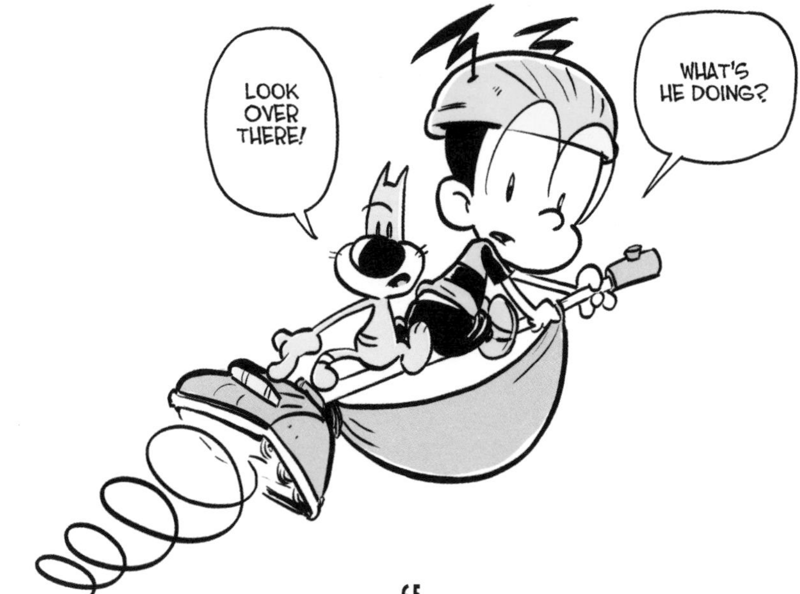
WHAT'S HE DOING?
LOOK OVER THERE!

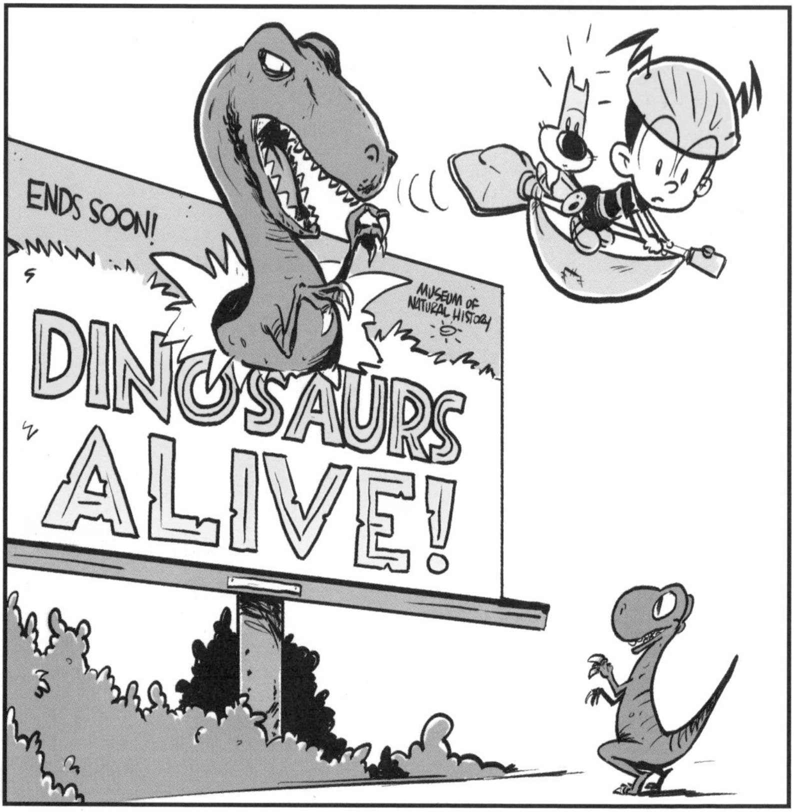
ENDS SOON!
MUSEUM OF NATURAL HISTORY
DINOSAURS ALIVE!

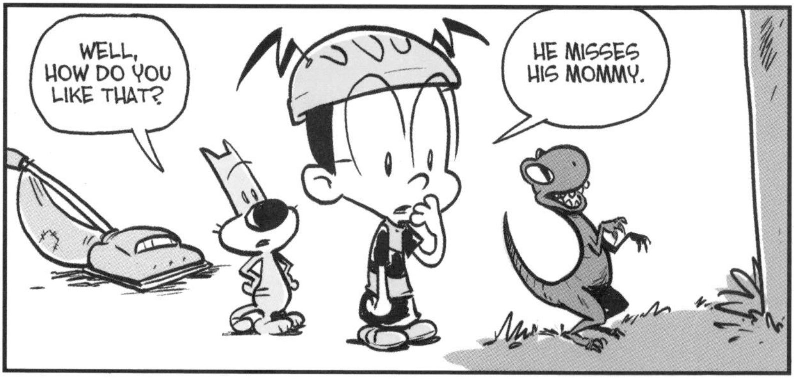
WELL, HOW DO YOU LIKE THAT?
HE MISSES HIS MOMMY.

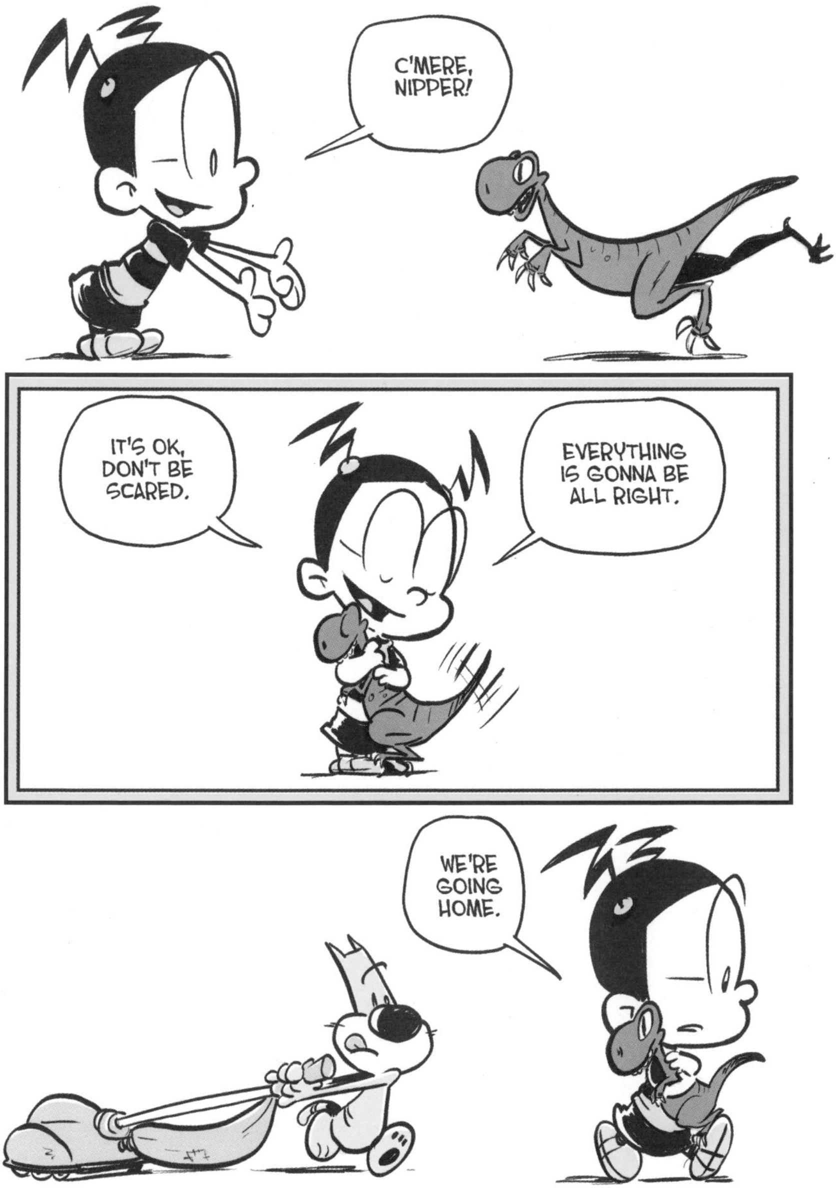
C'MERE, NIPPER!
IT'S OK, DON'T BE SCARED.
EVERYTHING IS GONNA BE ALL RIGHT.
WE'RE GOING HOME.

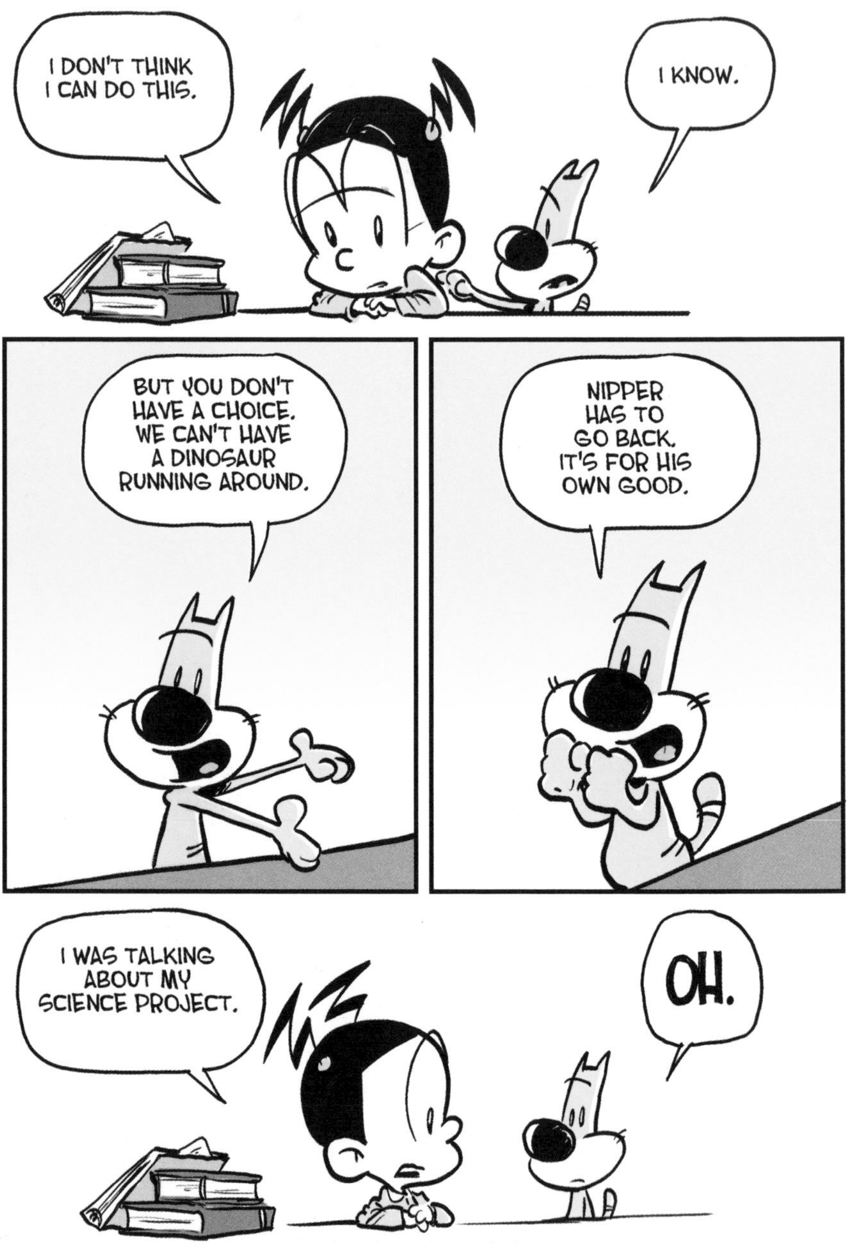
I DON'T THINK I CAN DO THIS.
I KNOW.
BUT YOU DON'T HAVE A CHOICE. WE CAN'T HAVE A DINOSAUR RUNNING AROUND.
NIPPER HAS TO GO BACK. IT'S FOR HIS OWN GOOD.
I WAS TALKING ABOUT MY SCIENCE PROJECT.
OH.

Getting to Know... Nipper

LIKES

- HUGS
- CHEESE DOODLES
- PLAYING FETCH

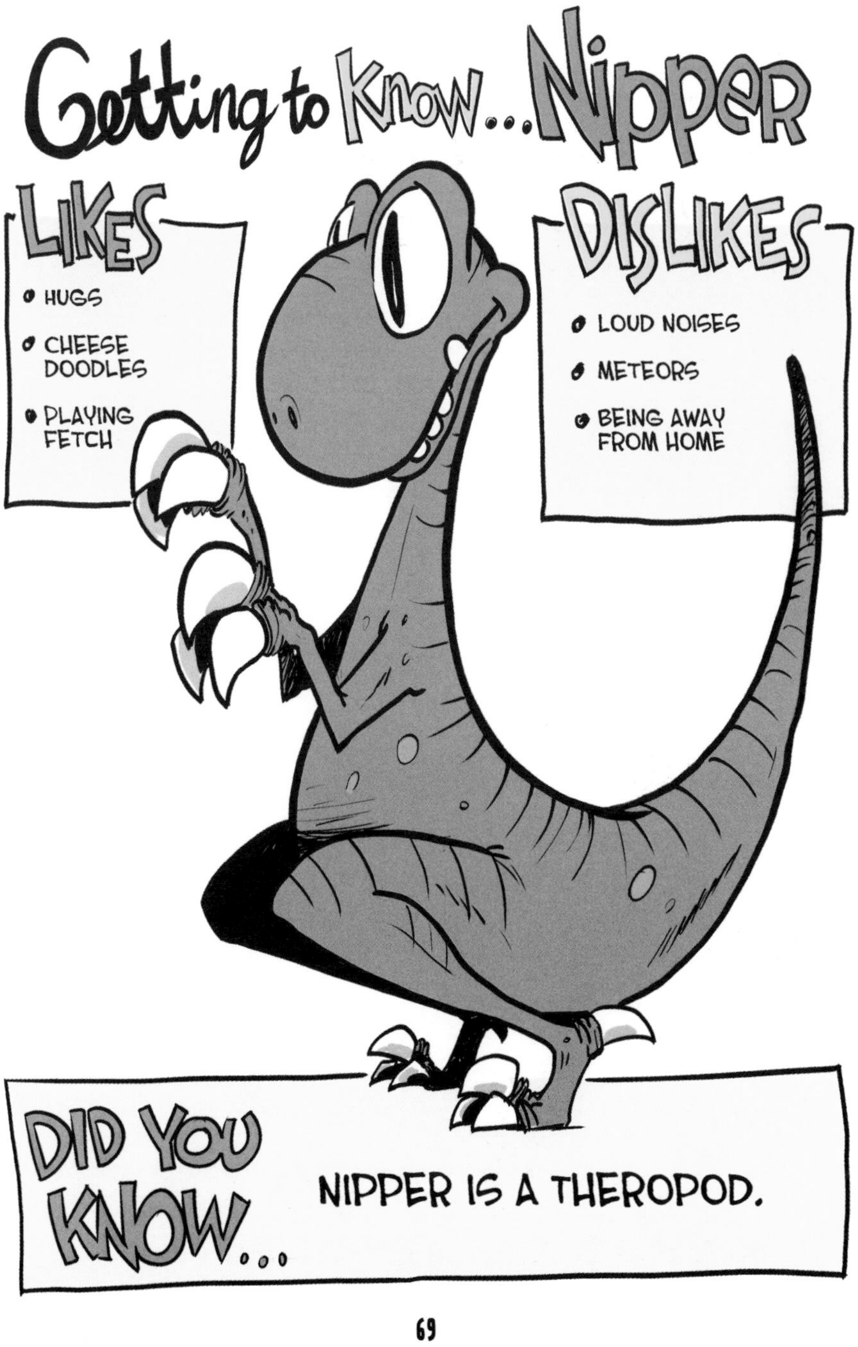

DISLIKES

- LOUD NOISES
- METEORS
- BEING AWAY FROM HOME

DID YOU KNOW...

NIPPER IS A THEROPOD.

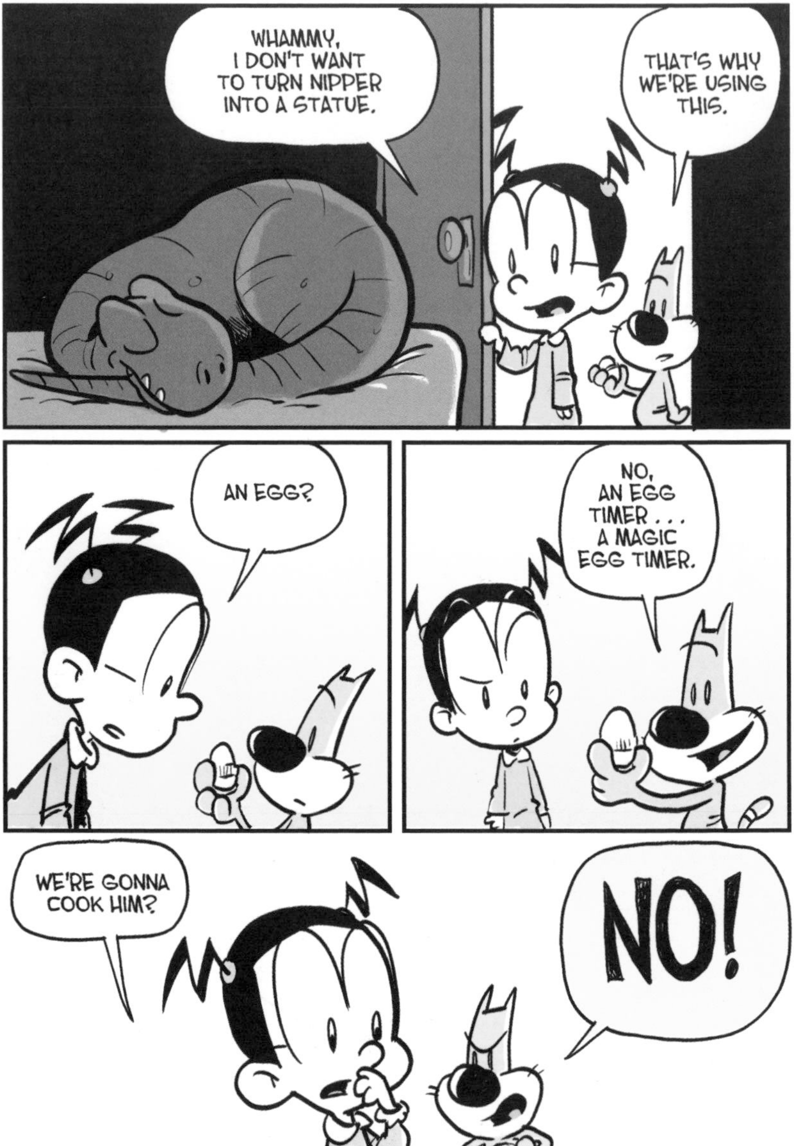
WHAMMY, I DON'T WANT TO TURN NIPPER INTO A STATUE.
THAT'S WHY WE'RE USING THIS.
AN EGG?
NO, AN EGG TIMER . . . A MAGIC EGG TIMER.
WE'RE GONNA COOK HIM?
NO!

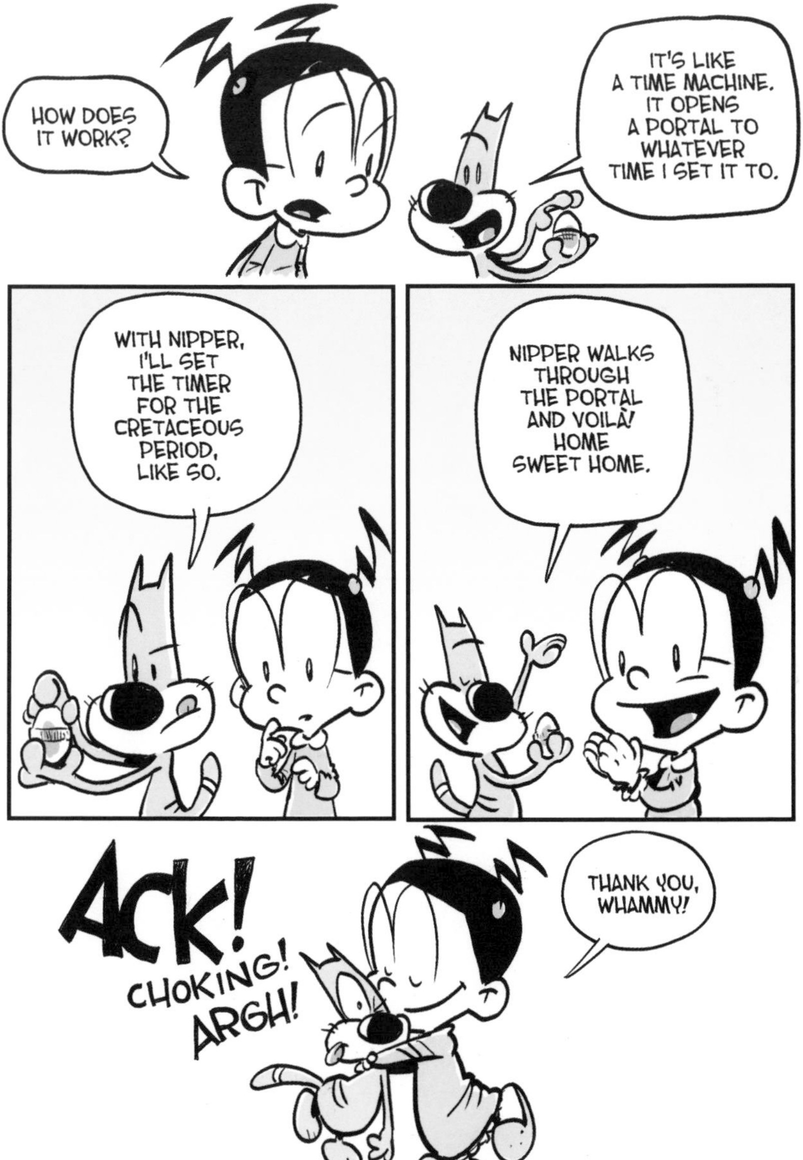
HOW DOES IT WORK?
IT'S LIKE A TIME MACHINE. IT OPENS A PORTAL TO WHATEVER TIME I SET IT TO.
WITH NIPPER, I'LL SET THE TIMER FOR THE CRETACEOUS PERIOD, LIKE SO.
NIPPER WALKS THROUGH THE PORTAL AND VOILÀ! HOME SWEET HOME.
ACK!
CHOKING!
ARGH!
THANK YOU, WHAMMY!

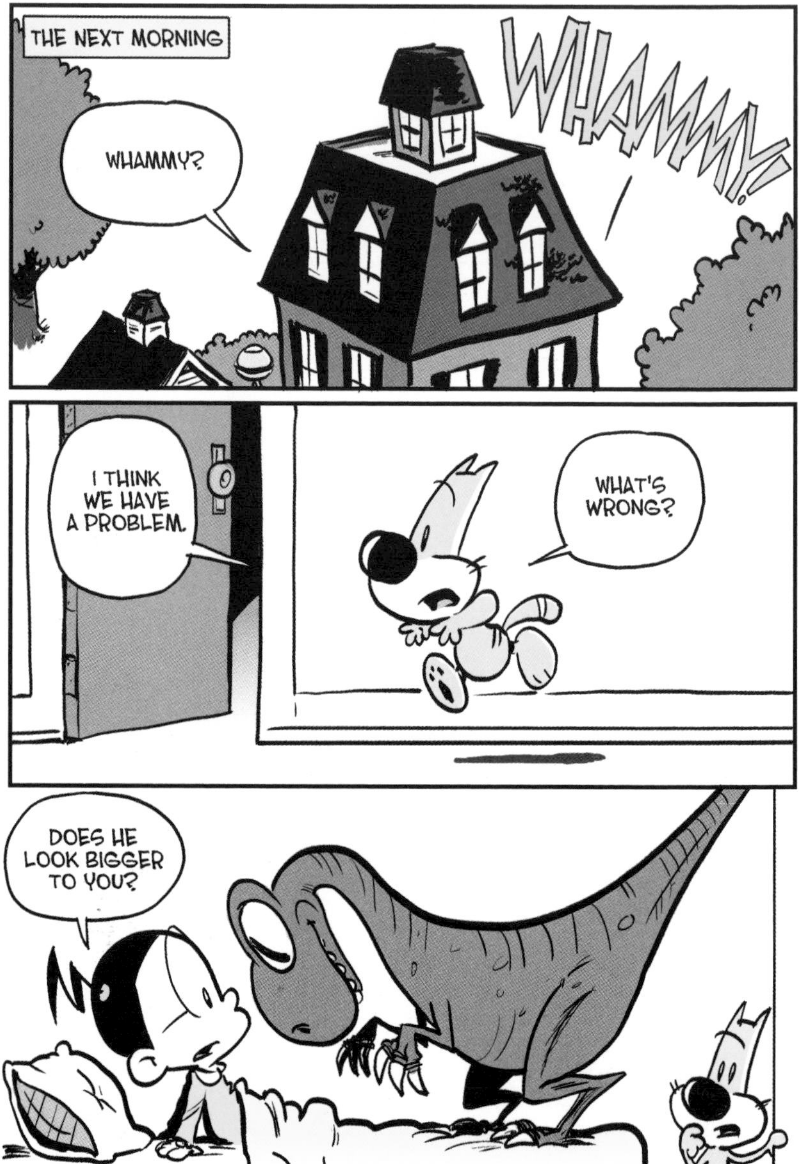
THE NEXT MORNING
WHAMMY!
WHAMMY?
I THINK WE HAVE A PROBLEM.
WHAT'S WRONG?
DOES HE LOOK BIGGER TO YOU?

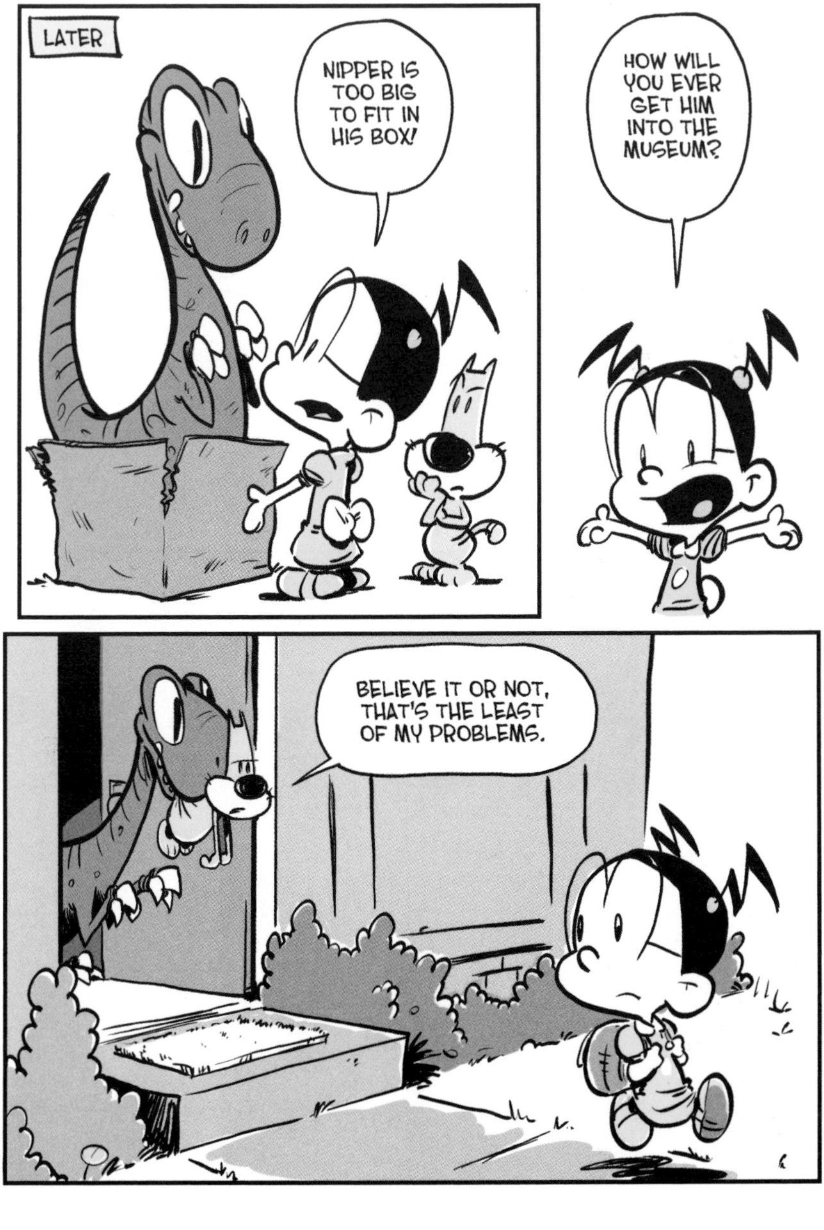
LATER
NIPPER IS TOO BIG TO FIT IN HIS BOX!
HOW WILL YOU EVER GET HIM INTO THE MUSEUM?
BELIEVE IT OR NOT, THAT'S THE LEAST OF MY PROBLEMS.

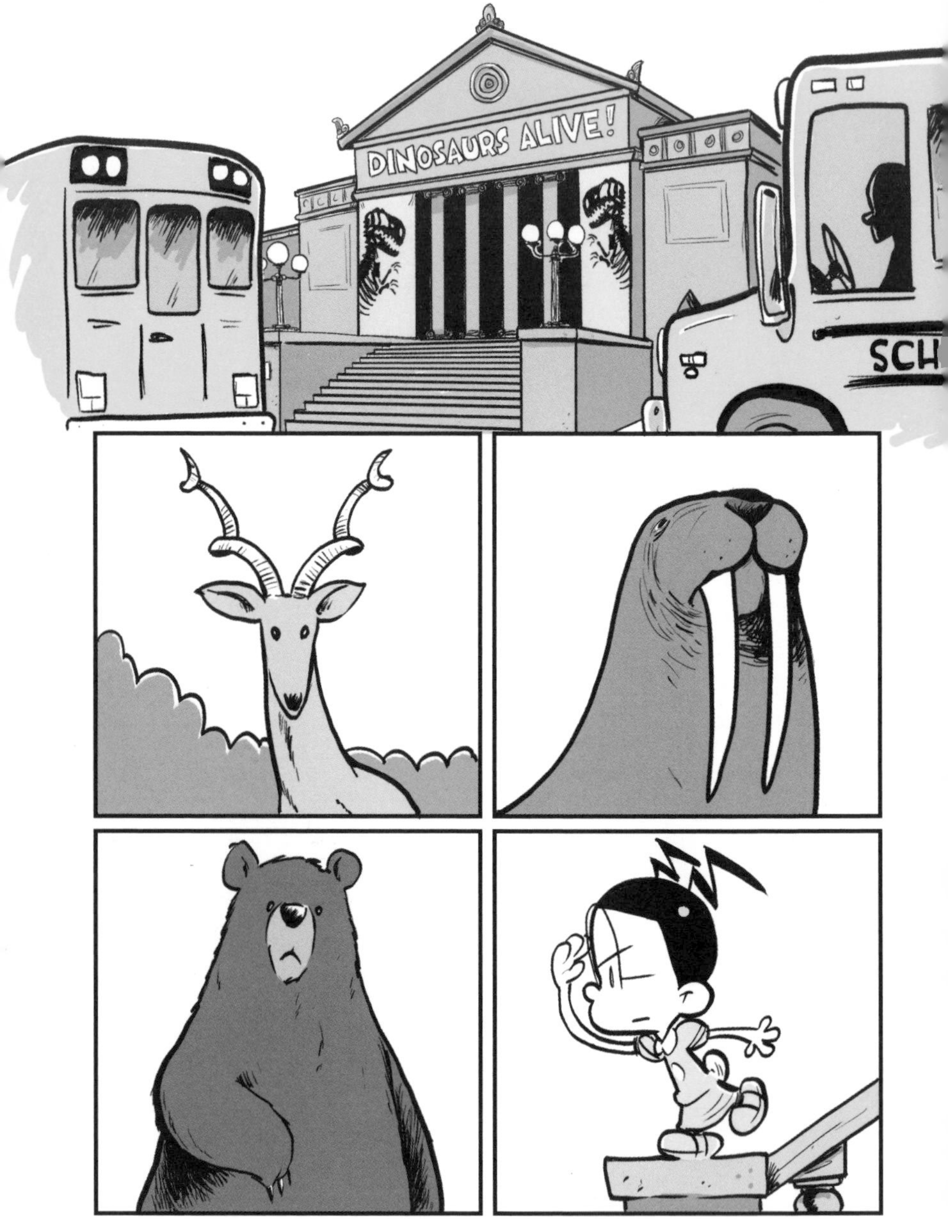

DINOSAURS ALIVE!
SCH

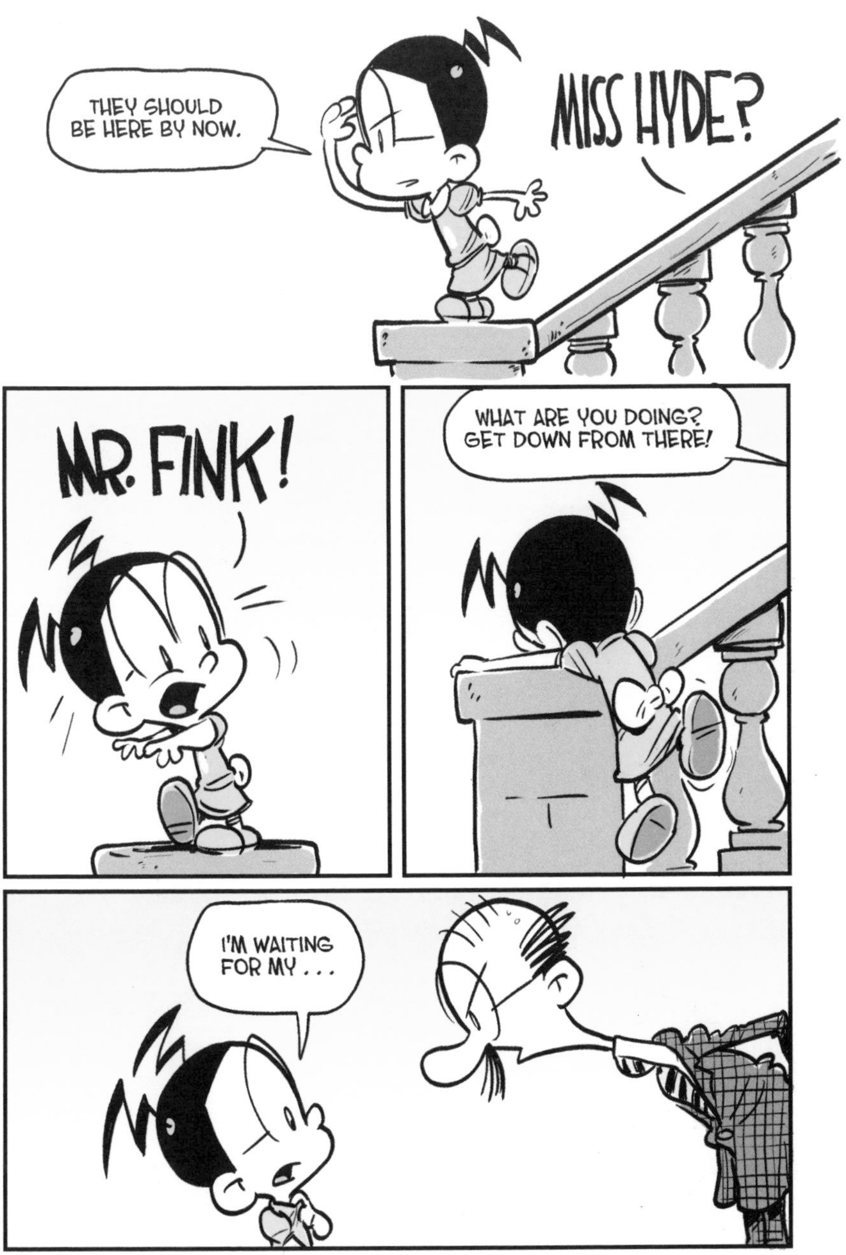
THEY SHOULD BE HERE BY NOW.
MISS HYDE?
MR. FINK!
WHAT ARE YOU DOING? GET DOWN FROM THERE!
I'M WAITING FOR MY . . .

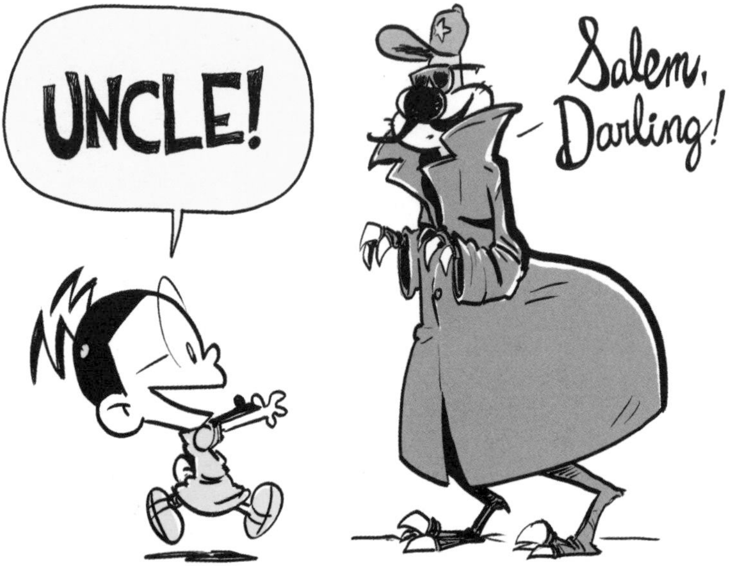
UNCLE!
Salem, Darling!

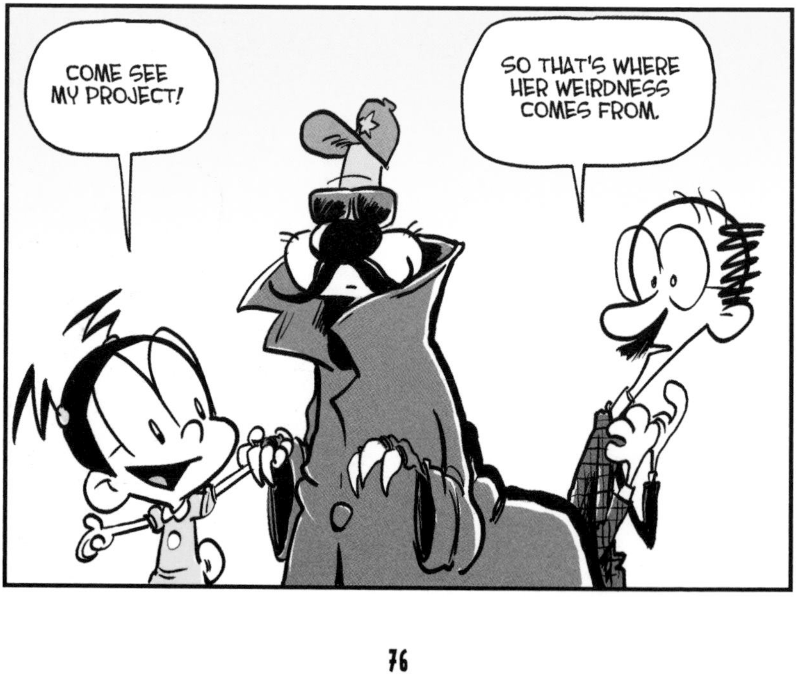
COME SEE MY PROJECT!
SO THAT'S WHERE HER WEIRDNESS COMES FROM.

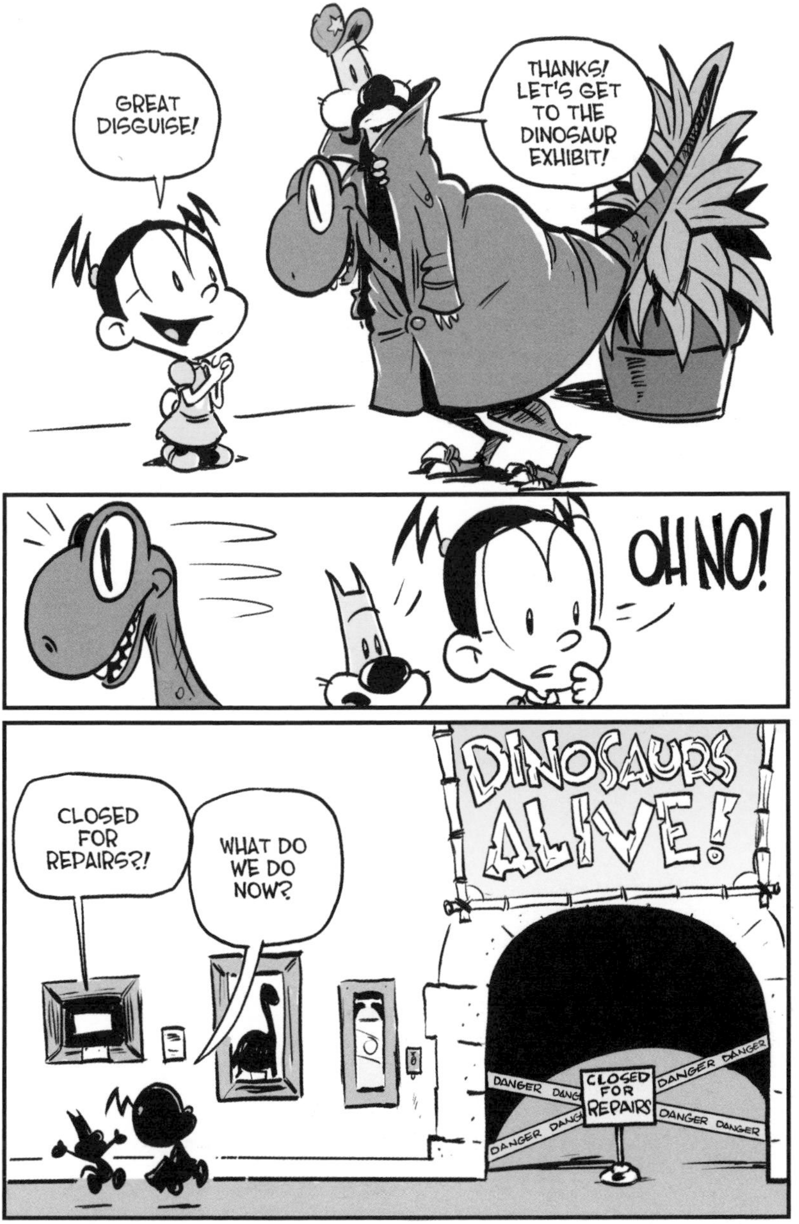
GREAT DISGUISE!
THANKS! LET'S GET TO THE DINOSAUR EXHIBIT!
OH NO!
DINOSAURS ALIVE!
CLOSED FOR REPAIRS?!
WHAT DO WE DO NOW?
DANGER DANGER
CLOSED FOR REPAIRS
DANGER DANGER

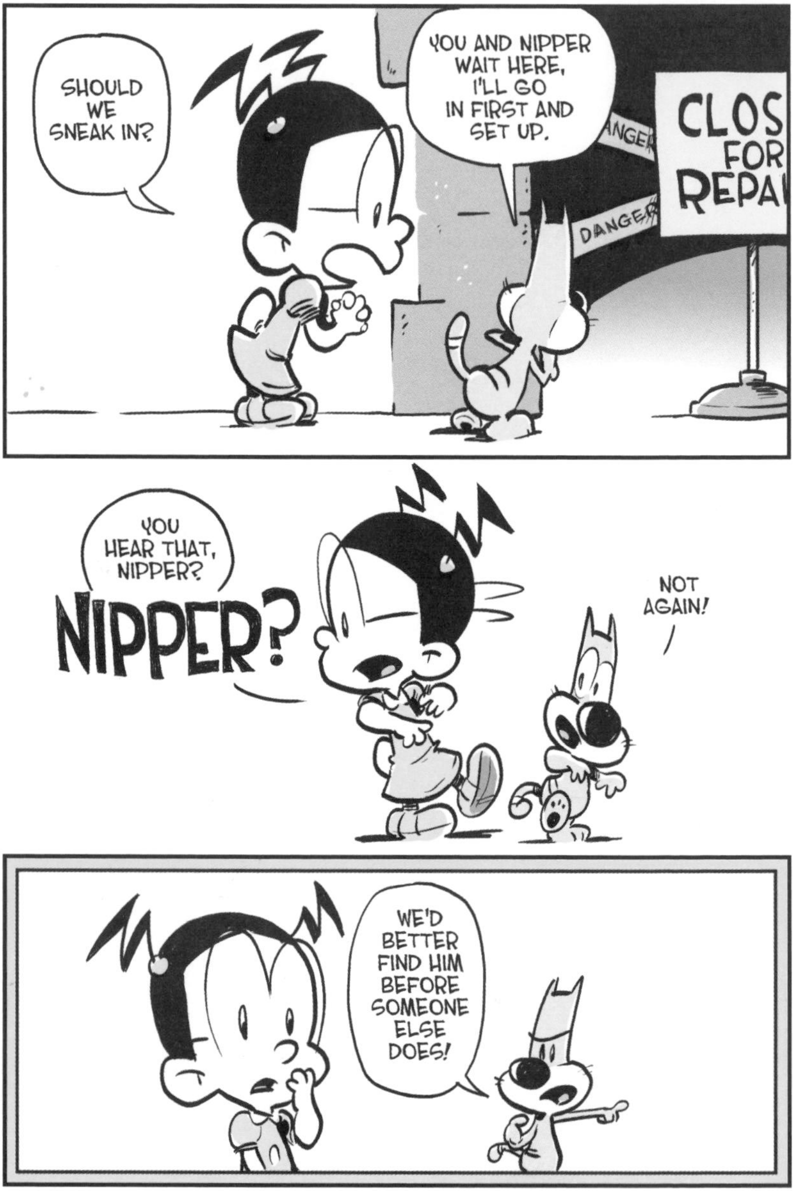
SHOULD WE SNEAK IN?
YOU AND NIPPER WAIT HERE, I'LL GO IN FIRST AND SET UP.
DANGER
DANGER
CLOS FOR REPA
YOU HEAR THAT, NIPPER?
NIPPER?
NOT AGAIN!
WE'D BETTER FIND HIM BEFORE SOMEONE ELSE DOES!

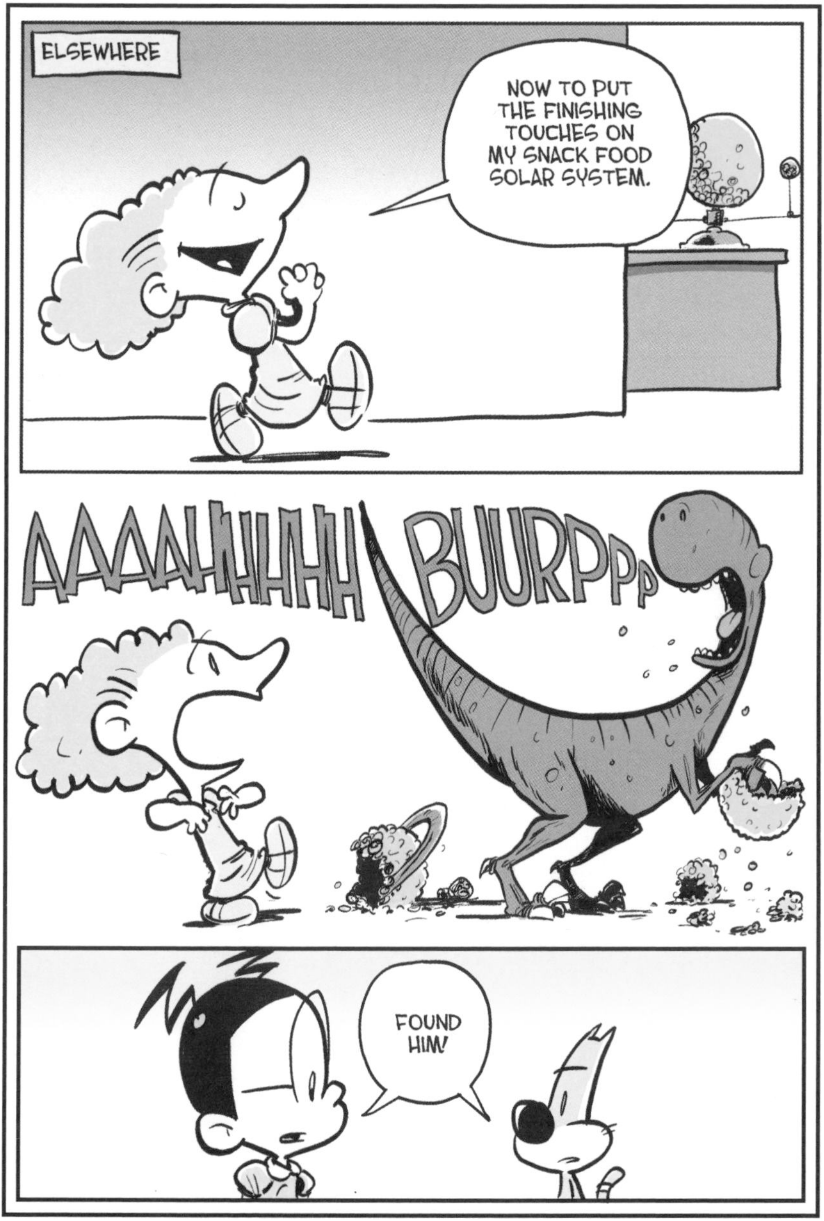
ELSEWHERE
NOW TO PUT THE FINISHING TOUCHES ON MY SNACK FOOD SOLAR SYSTEM.
AAAAHHHHH
BUURPPP
FOUND HIM!

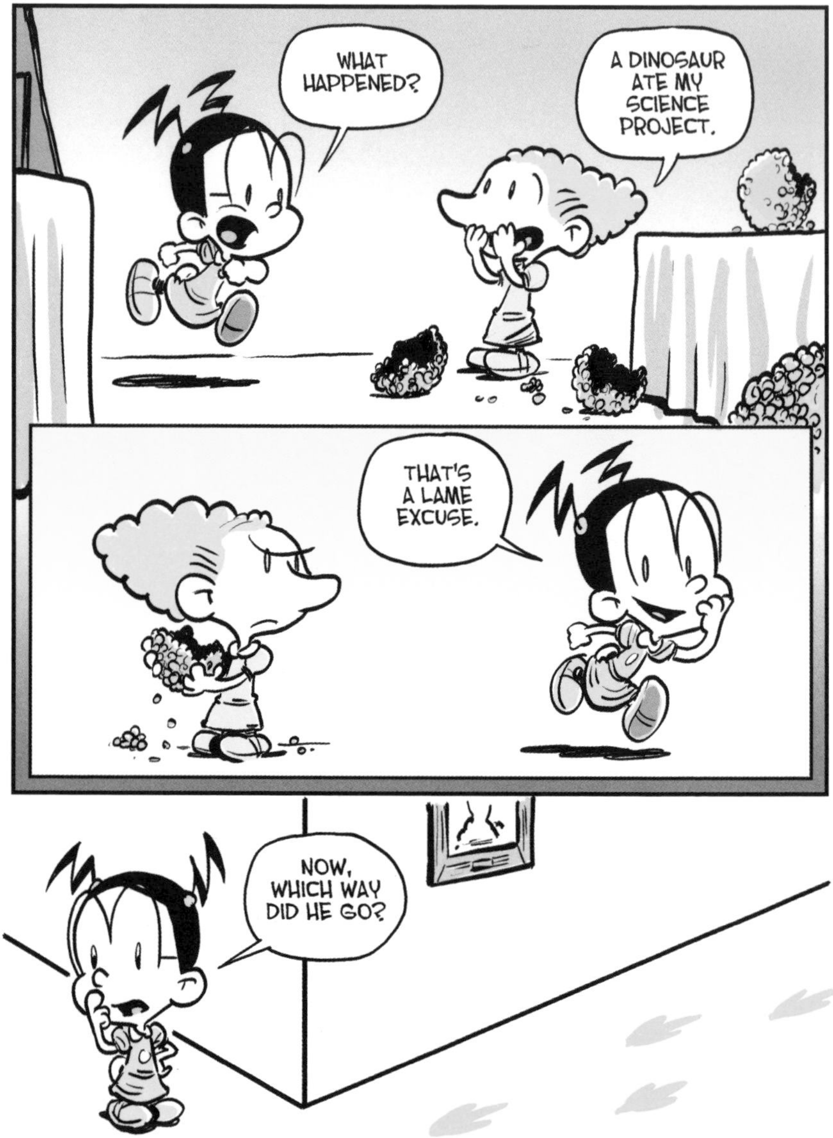
WHAT HAPPENED?
A DINOSAUR ATE MY SCIENCE PROJECT.
THAT'S A LAME EXCUSE.
NOW, WHICH WAY DID HE GO?

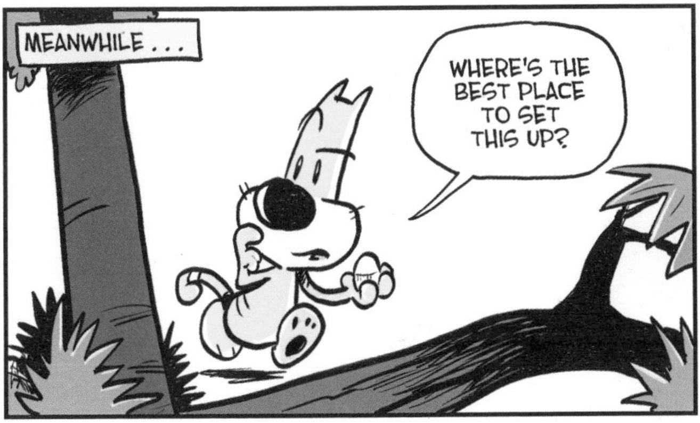
MEANWHILE . . .
WHERE'S THE BEST PLACE TO SET THIS UP?

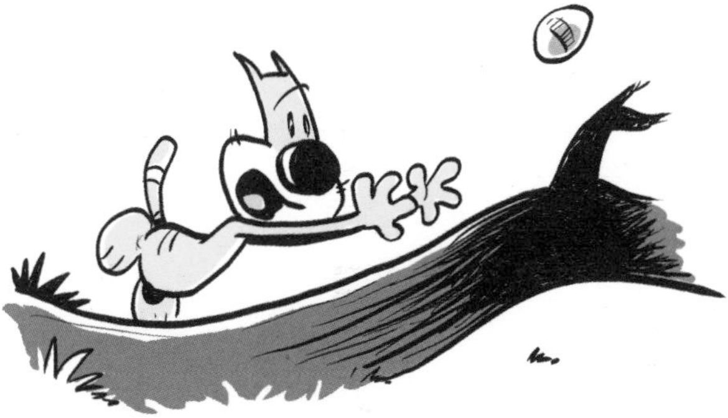

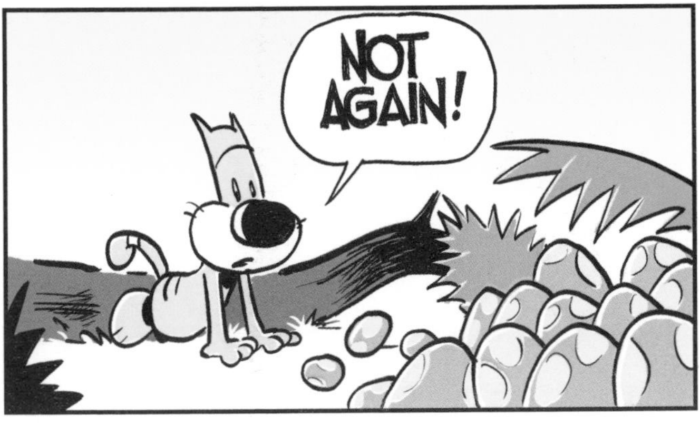
NOT AGAIN!

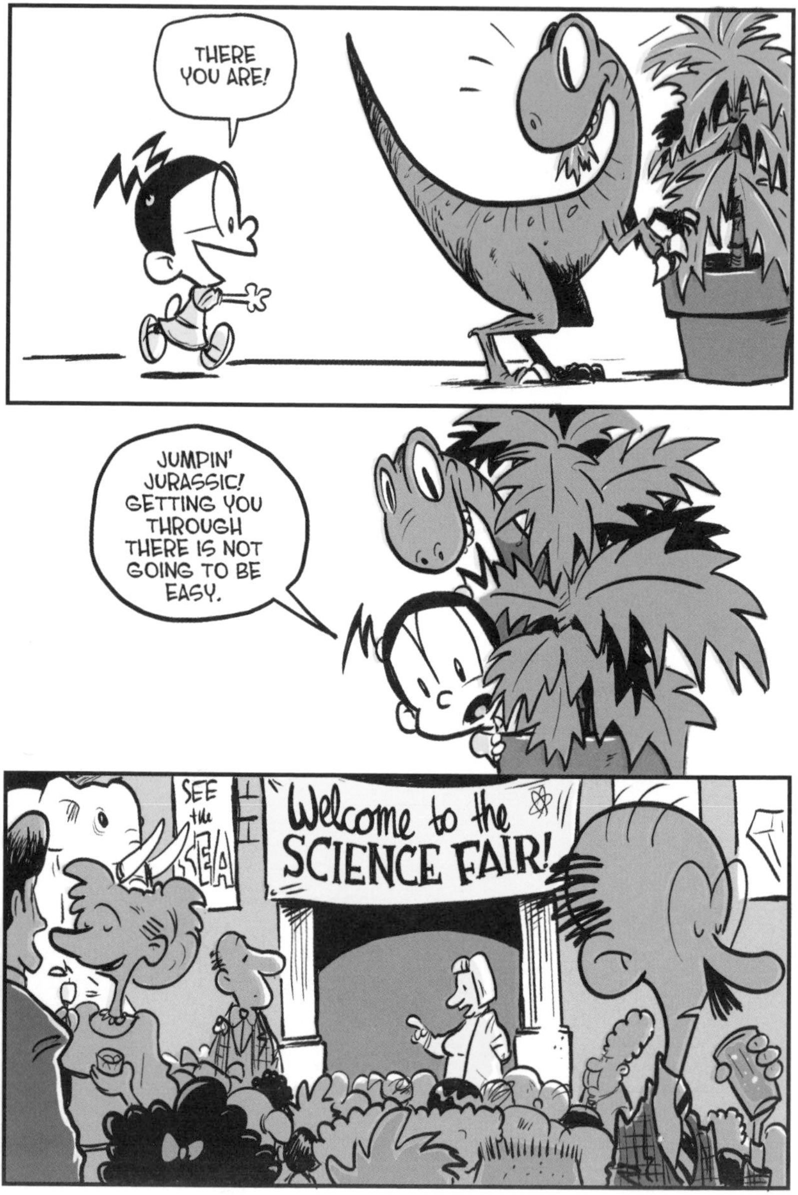
THERE YOU ARE!
JUMPIN' JURASSIC! GETTING YOU THROUGH THERE IS NOT GOING TO BE EASY.
SEE the
Welcome to the SCIENCE FAIR!

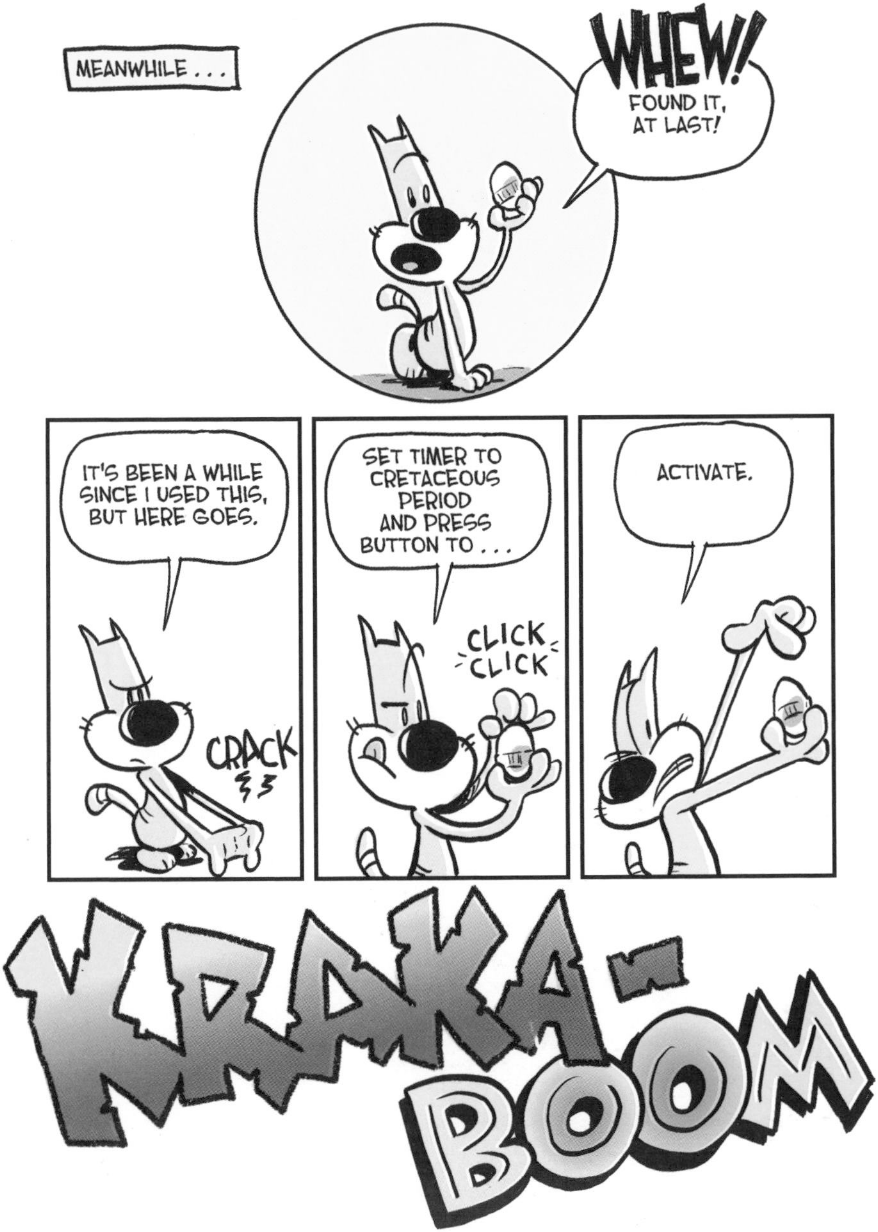
MEANWHILE . . .
WHEW! FOUND IT, AT LAST!
IT'S BEEN A WHILE SINCE I USED THIS, BUT HERE GOES.
CRACK
SET TIMER TO CRETACEOUS PERIOD AND PRESS BUTTON TO . . .
CLICK CLICK
ACTIVATE.
KRAKA-BOOM

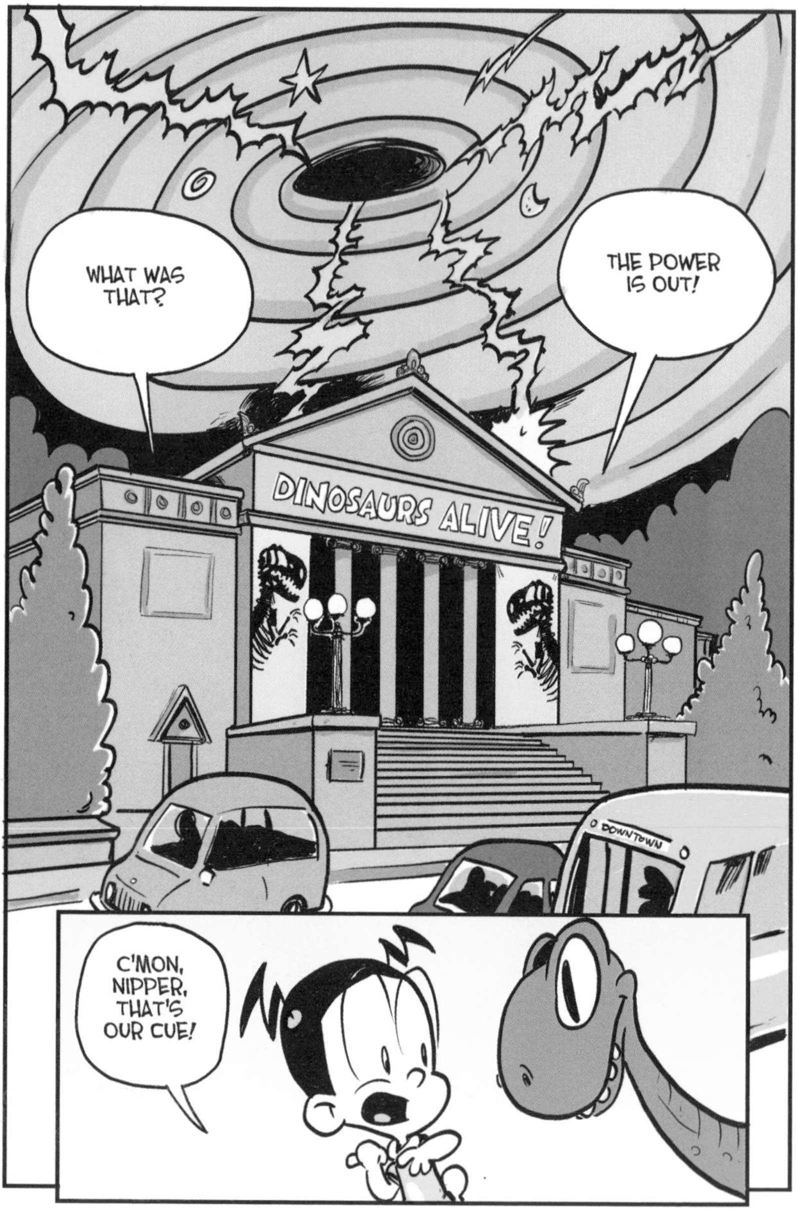
WHAT WAS THAT?
THE POWER IS OUT!
DINOSAURS ALIVE!
DOWNTOWN
C'MON, NIPPER, THAT'S OUR CUE!

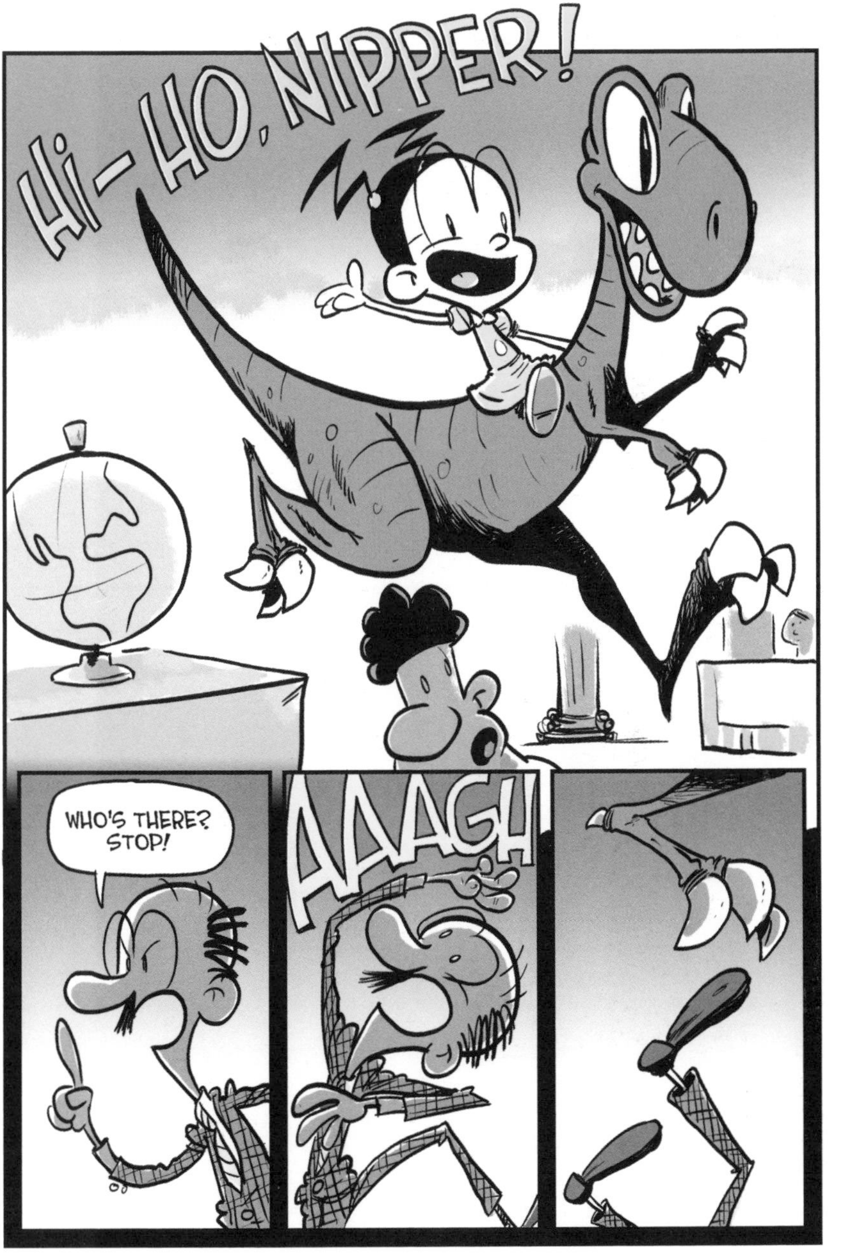
HI-HO, NIPPER!
WHO'S THERE? STOP!
AAAGH!

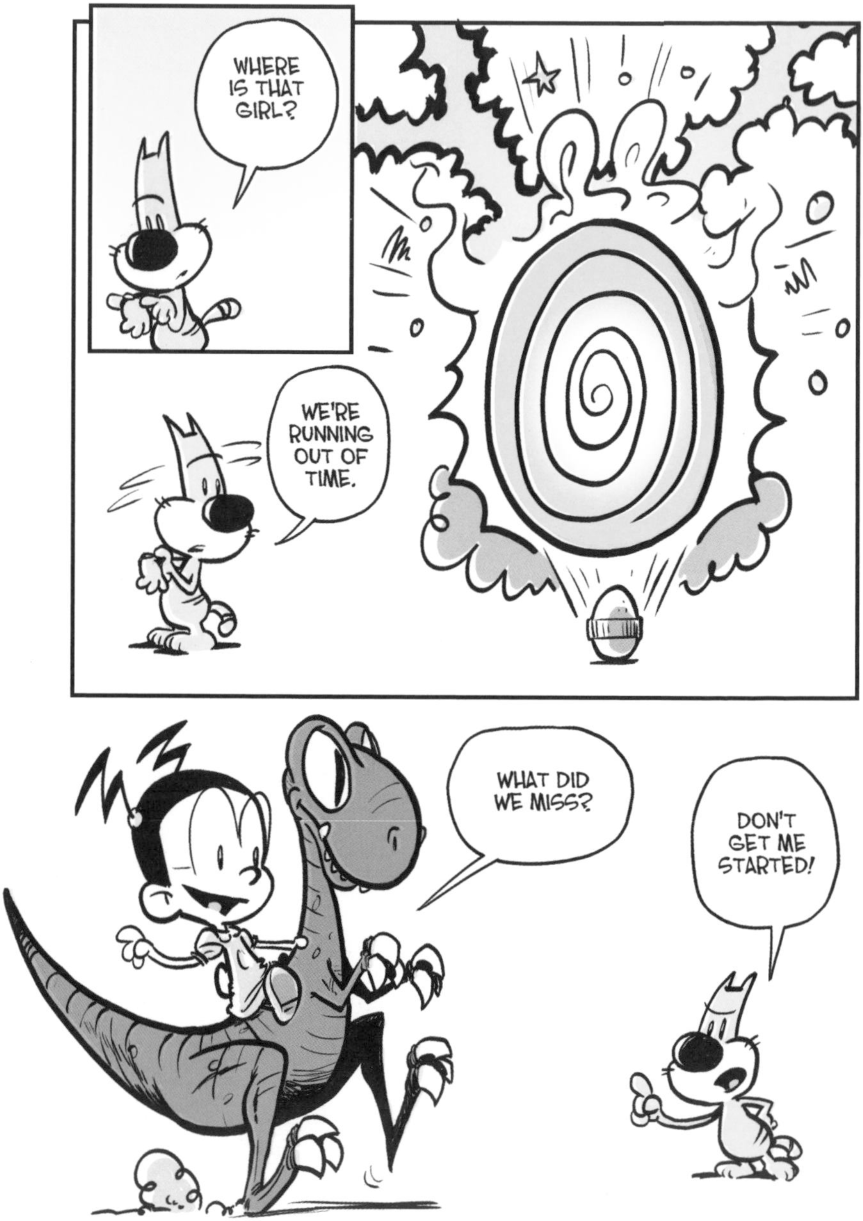
WHERE IS THAT GIRL?
WE'RE RUNNING OUT OF TIME.
WHAT DID WE MISS?
DON'T GET ME STARTED!

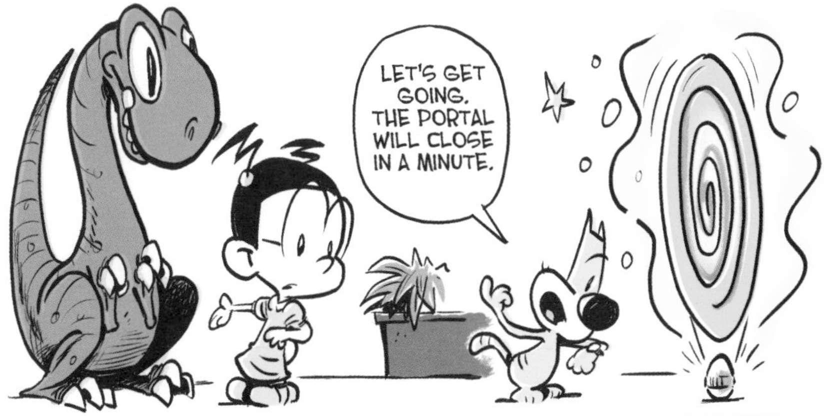
LET'S GET GOING. THE PORTAL WILL CLOSE IN A MINUTE.

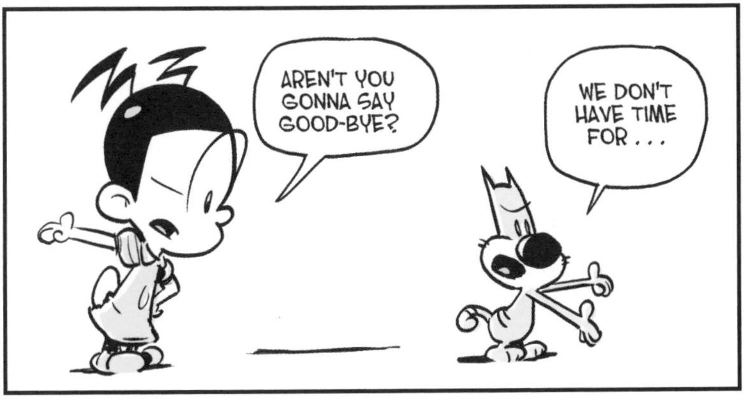
AREN'T YOU GONNA SAY GOOD-BYE?
WE DON'T HAVE TIME FOR . . .

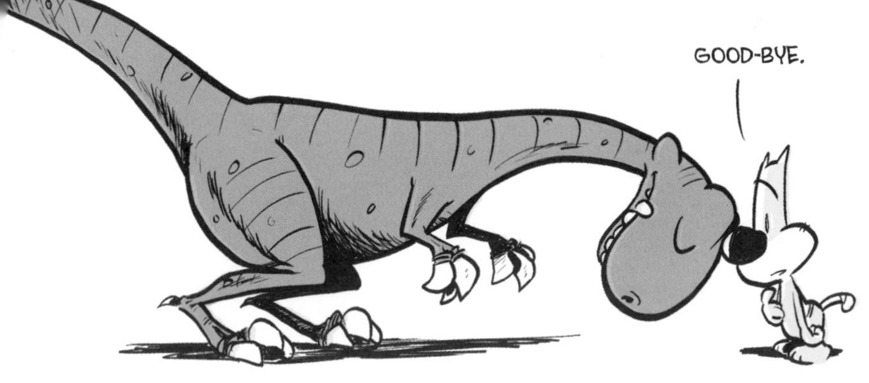
GOOD-BYE.

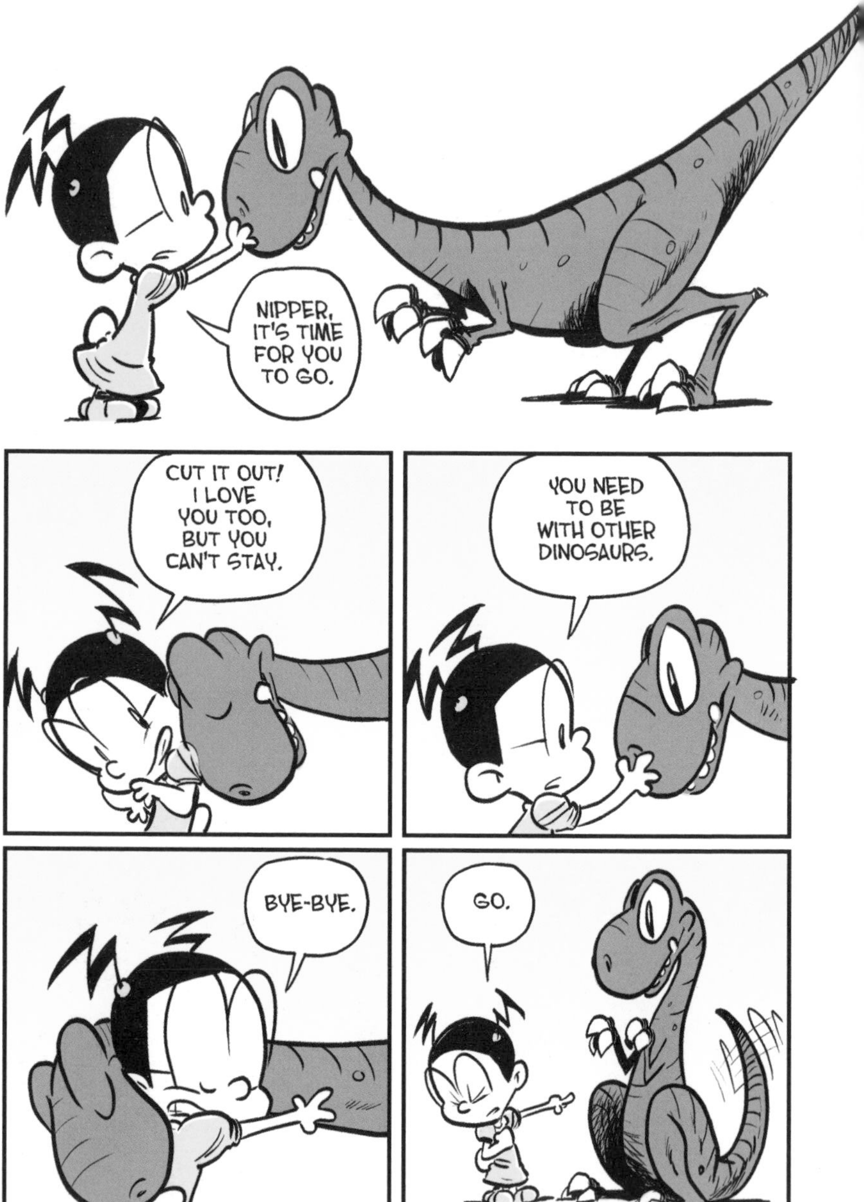
NIPPER, IT'S TIME FOR YOU TO GO.
CUT IT OUT! I LOVE YOU TOO, BUT YOU CAN'T STAY.
YOU NEED TO BE WITH OTHER DINOSAURS.
BYE-BYE.
GO.

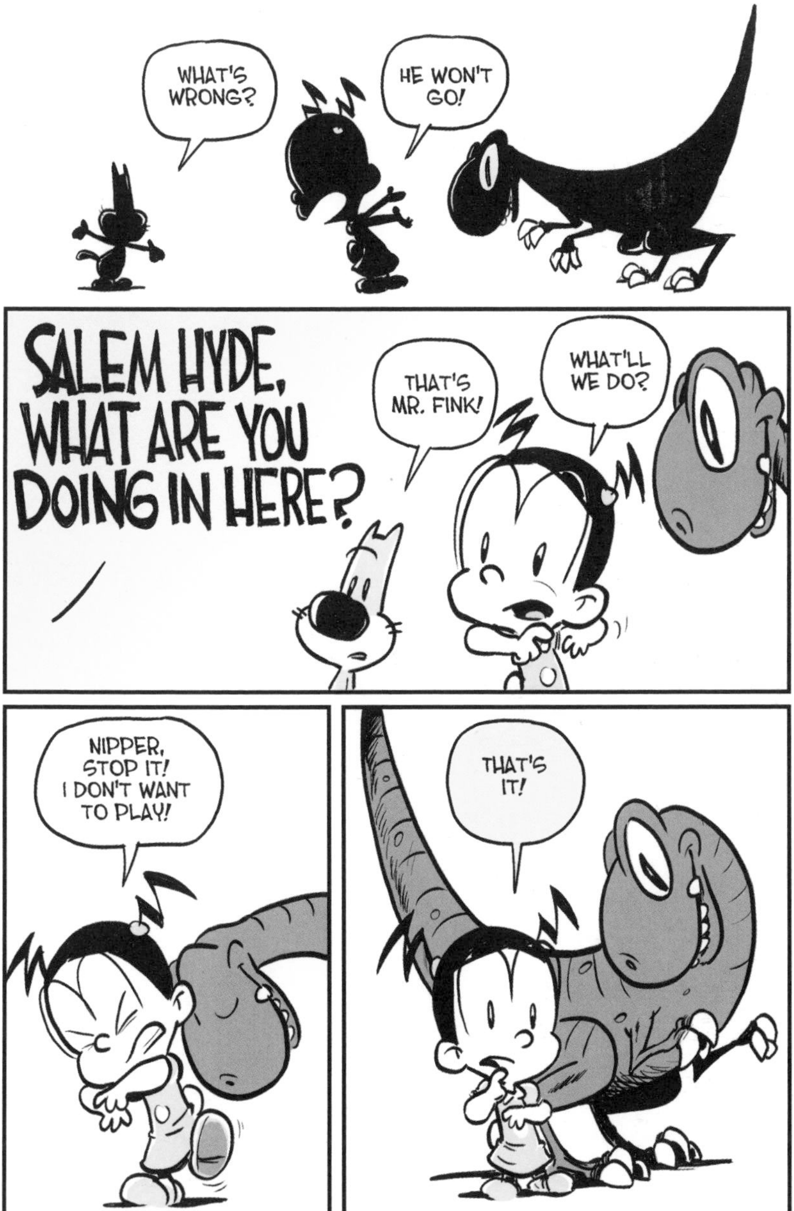
WHAT'S WRONG?
HE WON'T GO!
SALEM HYDE, WHAT ARE YOU DOING IN HERE?
THAT'S MR. FINK!
WHAT'LL WE DO?
NIPPER, STOP IT! I DON'T WANT TO PLAY!
THAT'S IT!

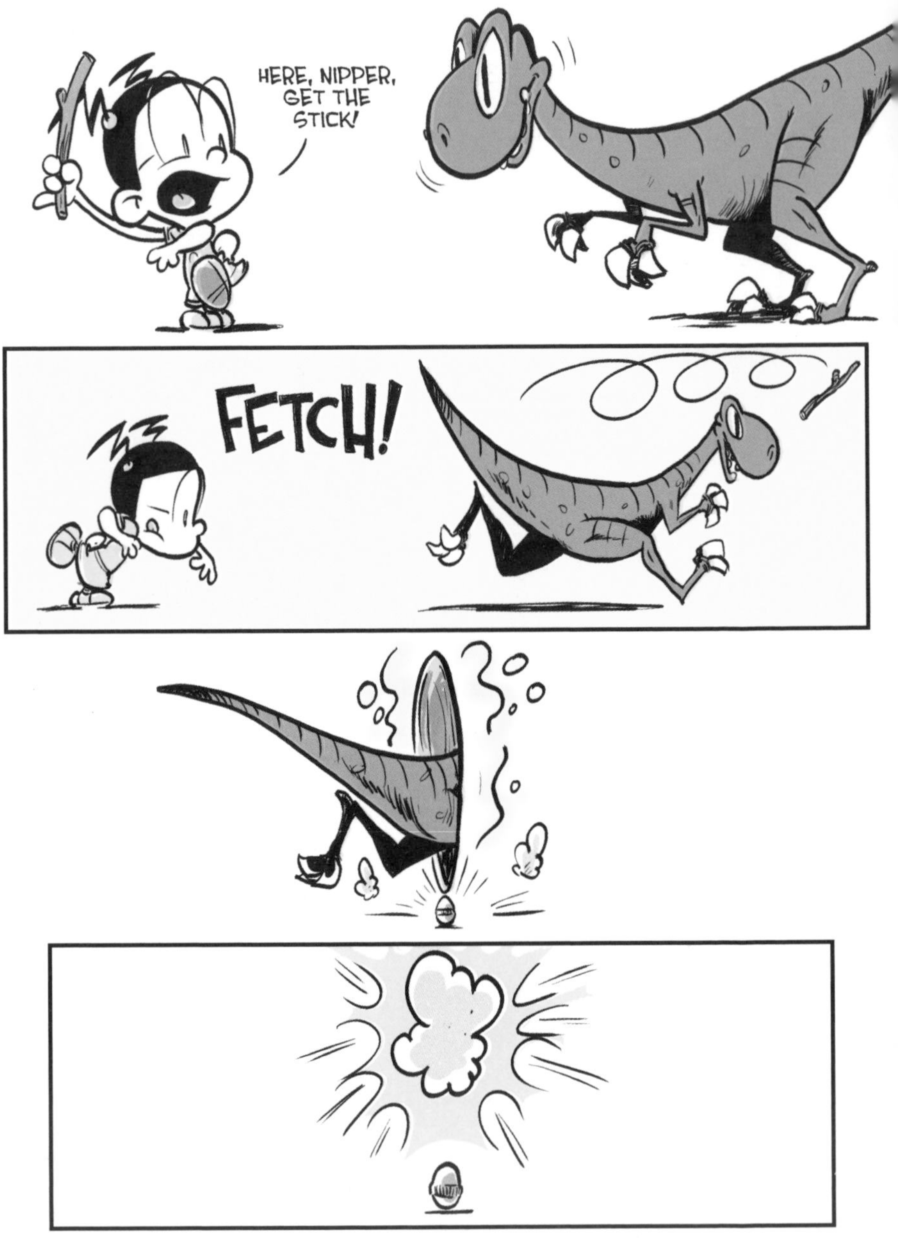
HERE, NIPPER, GET THE STICK!
FETCH!

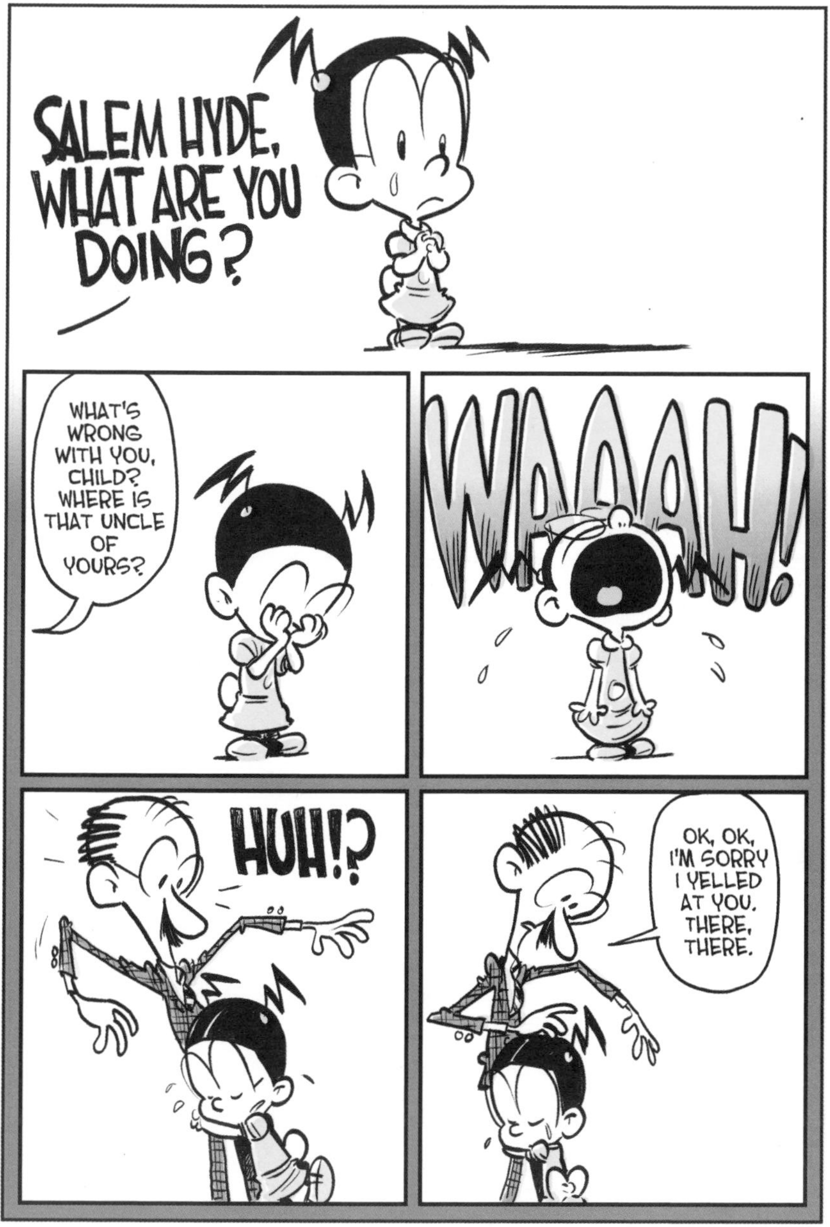
SALEM HYDE, WHAT ARE YOU DOING?
WHAT'S WRONG WITH YOU, CHILD? WHERE IS THAT UNCLE OF YOURS?
WAAAH!
HUH!?
OK, OK, I'M SORRY I YELLED AT YOU. THERE, THERE.

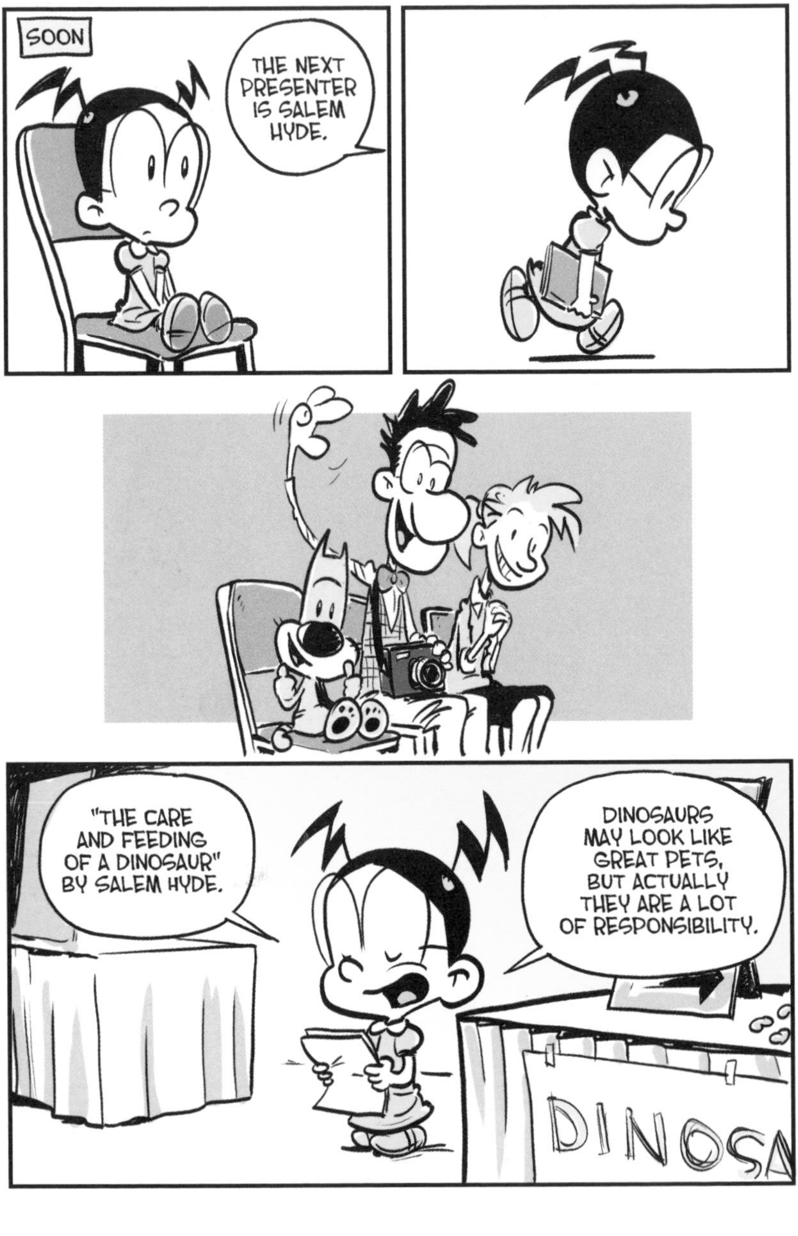
SOON
THE NEXT PRESENTER IS SALEM HYDE.
"THE CARE AND FEEDING OF A DINOSAUR" BY SALEM HYDE.
DINOSAURS MAY LOOK LIKE GREAT PETS, BUT ACTUALLY THEY ARE A LOT OF RESPONSIBILITY.
DINOSA

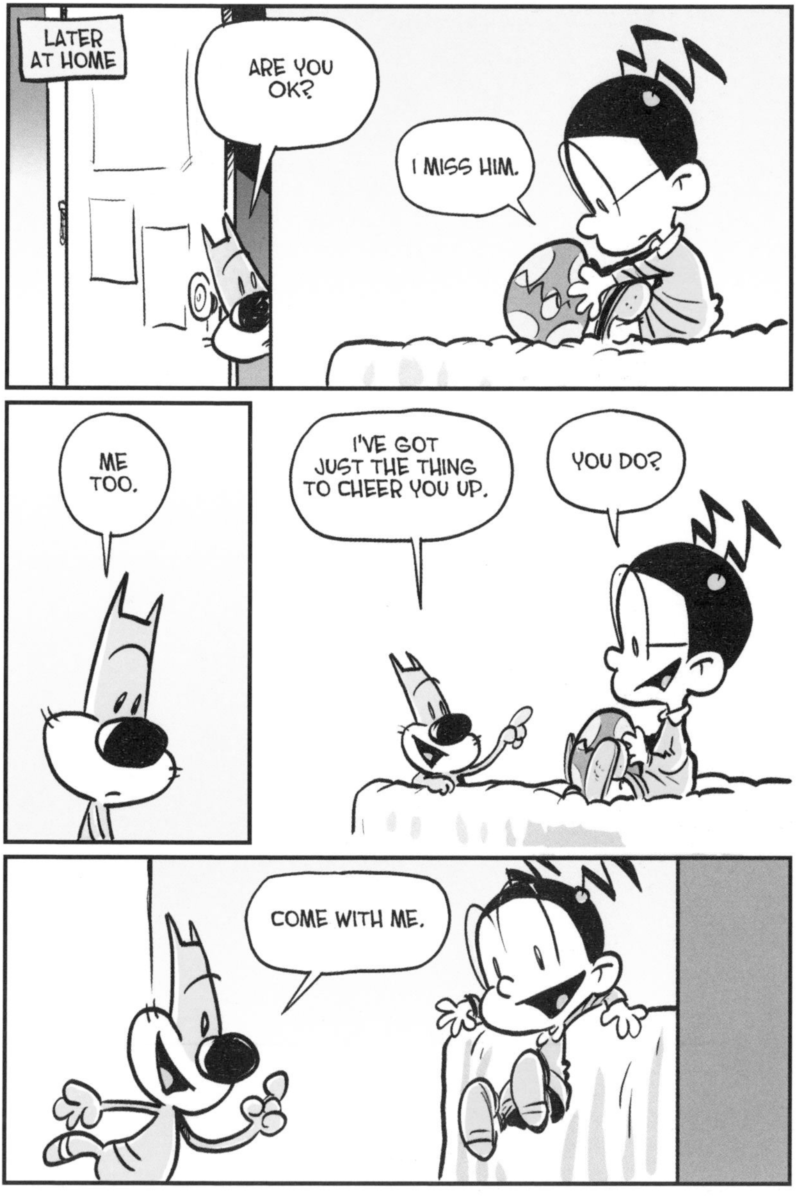
LATER AT HOME
ARE YOU OK?
I MISS HIM.
ME TOO.
I'VE GOT JUST THE THING TO CHEER YOU UP.
YOU DO?
COME WITH ME.

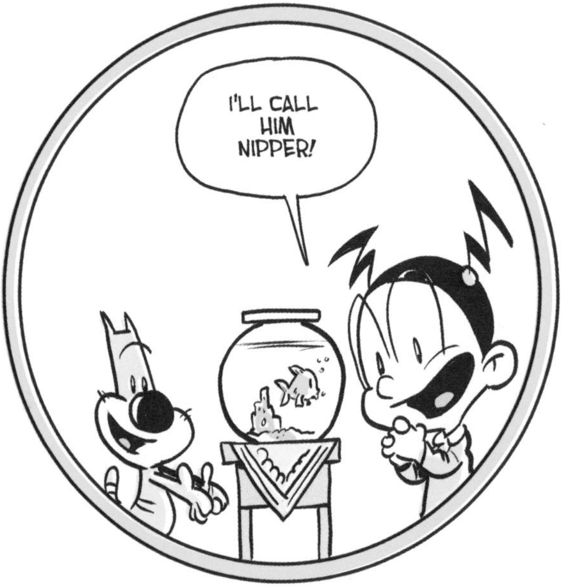
I'LL CALL
HIM
NIPPER!

Getting to Know FRANK CAMMUSO

FRANK LIKES
1. NATURAL HISTORY MUSEUMS
2. CHEESE DOODLES (ALL KINDS)
3. DRAWING DOODLES
4. FIELD TRIPS WITH HIS FAMILY

FRANK DISLIKES
1. SCIENCE PROJECTS
2. MAYONNAISE (ALL KINDS)
3. MOWING THE LAWN
4. CROWDS

FUN FACT: DID YOU KNOW ... THAT FRANK CAMMUSO'S FAVORITE DINOSAUR IS THE TRICERATOPS?

SPECIAL THANKS TO . . .

Ngoc and Khai, Kathy Leonardo, Nancy Iacovelli, Randy Elliott, Hart Seely, Tom Peyer, Nicole Sclama, Charlie Kochman, Chad Beckerman, Morgan Dubin, and Judy Hansen.

FOR MORE FUN STUFF ABOUT
SALEM AND WHAMMY
CHECK OUT MY WEBSITE AT . . .

WWW.CAMMUSO.COM

ALSO AVAILABLE

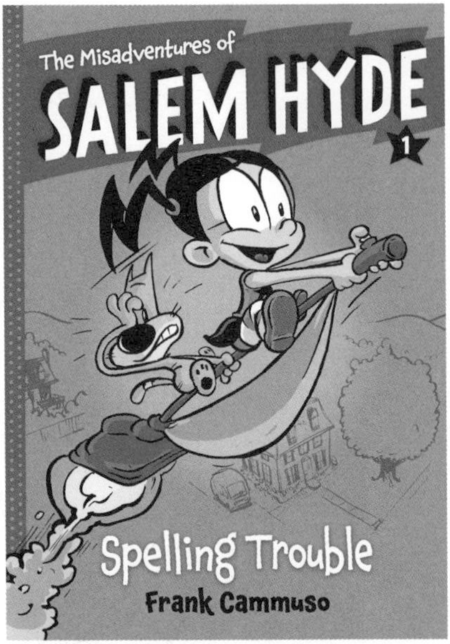

The Misadventures of
SALEM HYDE
1
Spelling Trouble
Frank Cammuso

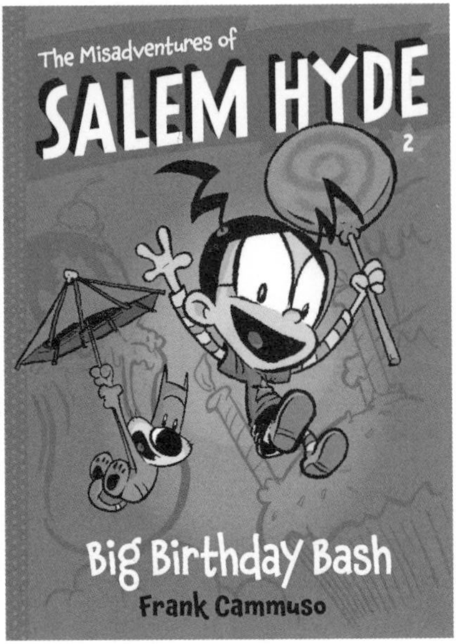

The Misadventures of
SALEM HYDE
2
Big Birthday Bash
Frank Cammuso

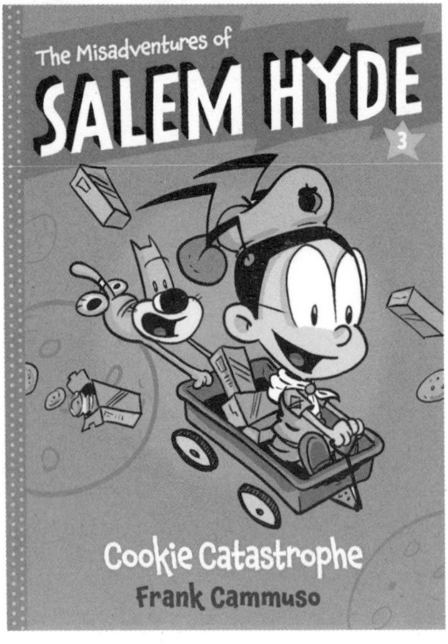

The Misadventures of
SALEM HYDE
3
Cookie Catastrophe
Frank Cammuso

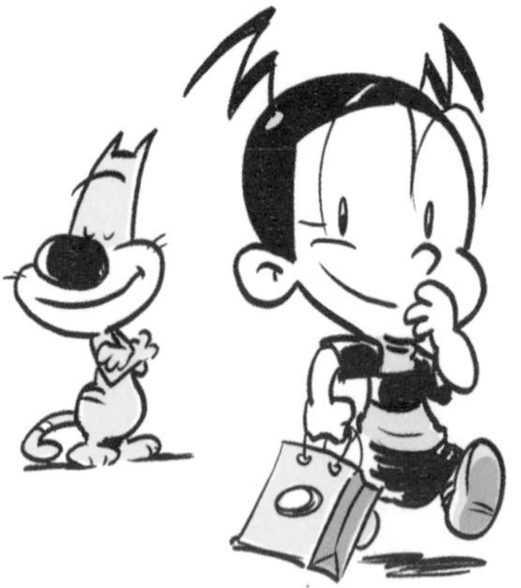

SALEM AND WHAMMY'S ADVENTURES WILL CONTINUE!